Dating the Funny Waitress

A Romantic Comedy Novel

ANGIE PEPPER

Chapter 1

Peridot Langtree's claim to fame was being a granddaughter of the famous country superstar Lana Langtree.

Peridot, or Perry to her friends, inherited none of her grandmother's singing ability, but all of her famous wit.

Perry's sassy attitude came in handy every day at Delilah's, a busy cafe on Baker Street. She was the youngest waitress there, but thanks to her attitude, she fit right in with the women who'd been there twenty years.

Perry's story began on Sunday, in the middle of the brunch rush.

Hungry customers were lined up down the block, as usual. The restaurant was slammed, and they were short a waitress.

Toph, one of the young guys from the kitchen, was attempting to help Perry and failing. He hovered too close, and he got in the way. His skinny body kept occupying the same space Perry was trying to pass through.

Perry finally said to the guy, "Toph, you lusty badger! I know you mean well, but if you slam your hips into me one more time, I'm going to call my dad to come down with his shotgun so we can get married, because that kind of hip-slamming is only appropriate for married people."

Toph responded by blushing furiously. Then he scurried back to the kitchen, which was what Perry wanted.

The line cook on the other side of the pass-through window raised his eyebrow at Perry. "Does your dad even own a shotgun?"

Perry winked at the cook. Channeling her famous grandmother's charm, she said, "Oh, sugar, he wishes! My papa's only allowed to handle the virtual ones that come in video games."

The cook rang the bell, even though Perry was standing right there. "Order up," he said.

Perry delivered the heavy plates then went to take the order of a table for two. The customers were a young couple who barely noticed she was there, let alone that she was run off her feet and dying for a washroom break.

The selfish, lovesick couple gazed into each other's eyes. Both of them had the damp hair of people who had recently showered together. Did they know how obvious they were? Everyone in the restaurant could tell that those two, who barely looked twenty, had woken up in the same bed together. Those lusty badgers!

Just standing there in their telltale pheromone bubble was making Perry's cheeks turn red the way Toph's had. She could talk the talk, but she had zero experience with love. Being around it made her deeply uncomfortable.

Perry dropped her gaze to avoid eye contact with the young lovers. It got worse. The couple were wearing matching sneakers.

As Perry Langtree stared at the matching sneakers—the sneakers that had also spent the night together like a couple of lusty badgers—the noise of the busy restaurant faded away.

A new, confusing sensation was bubbling up in Perry's chest.

Maybe it was the stress of serving fourteen tables by herself, or the tearful goodbye she'd had with her mother earlier that morning. Maybe Saturn was in retrograde, or the drizzly weather. Mostly it was the matching sneakers that had clearly, obviously, unashamedly spent the night together.

More of the feeling washed over her, but it wasn't accompanied by the usual nausea. That cute couple, on that particular Sunday, did not make Perry Langtree feel like barfing. Standing there, in the blast radius of their affection, she could feel what they had between them, and it wasn't making her hurl.

Love.

Suddenly, she wanted it.

She wanted to reach out and grab off a big chunk of it for herself. She wanted damp hair, matching sneakers, and giggling at each other while an overworked waitress waited for *her* order.

The couple eventually came out of their bliss enough to order.

Perry guessed how they wanted their eggs. "Over easy for both, right?"

The couple nodded then expressed surprise at each other. The dumb-dumbs didn't even know each other's egg preferences. That was how new their love was.

Perry was mildly relieved her egg-knowing superpowers weren't on the fritz. She jotted some squiggly lines on her notepad. In addition to knowing how people wanted their eggs, Perry could memorize everything for a table of ten, but she pretended to write the orders down anyway because it improved the tips. Perry was a show-off, but she was no fool about money.

She squeezed past Toph's skinny body. How was a guy as thin as him always in the way? He was back out front refilling coffee cups.

Perry shot him a warning look and punched in the new order for the kitchen.

Toph said, "Please don't kill me, Perry. Donny told me to come back out and help."

"We're cool," she said. "Thanks for helping."

"You know... I would," Toph said, grinning. "Marry you. If you wanted."

"Keep your pants on." She hip-checked him out of the way and put on a fresh pot of coffee. "Hey, Toph, do you remember puberty?"

He laughed nervously. "I'm not sure I'm out of it yet."

"Do you remember having dreams about putting on your pajamas and going to visit other kids from your class, and seeing them in their pajamas?"

Toph stopped scraping plates for the dishwasher and stared at her. "Are you joking?"

"Never mind," she said.

"Pajama meetups? Is that what passes for a sex dream in Peridot Langtree's world?"

"Ew. Don't say my full name, you creepy weirdo. And don't ever think about my dreams ever again. Forget I said anything."

"Perry, have you even been with a guy?"

She jabbed her finger at him. "This is not appropriate workplace conversation."

"You started it." Toph was beaming now. This was the most fun he'd ever had working at Delilah's, and that was saying something because the kitchen crew got up to some pretty spectacular shenanigans.

She stepped toward him, hissing like an angry cat.

Toph didn't even flinch.

The order bell rang.

Perry grabbed the plates and returned to the floor, where she took out her mood on the customers. But it was okay. Delilah's was one of those places where the waitresses were encouraged to get sassy with the customers. Some of the older ladies, like Maggie, didn't put in much effort anymore, but Perry worked there mainly because she loved that aspect of the job.

When the food order came up for Matching Sneakers, she really let them have it.

"Okay, dumb-dumbs," she said to them, loudly. "If you could spread around your digital devices and other crap more evenly, I can dump these plates on top of everything and you can start chowing down."

The couple stared up at her in shock. They didn't move their stuff.

A silence spread out around Perry and the table of two. Everyone was listening. This was the sort of moment Perry lived for. She didn't have her famous grandmother's singing voice, but she had inherited Lana's flair for performance.

"Any time you're ready," Perry said. "I'm not sure what you heard about this place, but the waitresses don't have mutant superpowers in their hands. Your food's not getting any hotter with me holding it here. Well? Did you come here to eat, or to play footsie with your matching sneakers?"

Some tourist-types at the next table snickered. Two tables away, Little Miss Soft-Poached got out her phone to capture the magic.

The lovesick couple unfroze and jerkily moved their phones and books out of the way.

Perry dropped the plates with a loud clatter. "Eat up fast," she said. "Our tables are small because it discourages riffraff like you from lingering."

There was a smattering of applause.

Another diner turned around and told the couple, "At Delilah's, the attitude is all part of the experience. Feel free to whistle or snap your fingers if you want the abuse to escalate."

Matching Sneaker Girl said, "Right! I heard about that, but I totally forgot. We don't get over to Baker Street much."

"We live over on Hurst," the Matching Sneaker Guy said.

"West siders," Perry said with disgust, as though that explained everything. "Hurst is the worst. There's a dollar surcharge for you having crossed over Parker Street into the exotic East. I'll waive it today since it's your first time and at least you're not wearing yoga pants."

"We don't do yoga," the girl said.

Perry replied sternly, "Ma'am, I'll be adding a two-dollar surcharge for lying."

The customers who'd been listening in roared with laughter.

Matching Sneakers Guy said to his sweetheart, "Just eat. You're only making it worse."

The order-up bell rang, and Perry went off to do the boring part of her job.

She continued to torture the young lovers even more by being extra-nice to everyone else around them.

They tipped generously, as she'd known they would.

Chapter 2

Monday

Perry Langtree was glad it was Monday.

Monday would be much better than Sunday because there wouldn't be any gross lovesick couples having brunch. It wasn't raining, so everyone coming in that morning would have bone-dry hair. Instead of damply radiating love pheromones, all the tables for two would only broadcast a strong need for coffee refills.

Delilah's was still empty, with the first of the Monday morning breakfast customers not there yet.

Perry's best friend and coworker, Courtney Liu, was filling the ketchup bottles with a funnel. Courtney was five feet of seemingly effortless chic, from her shiny black hair, cut in an asymmetrical bob, to her chunky footwear. Courtney had a self-assuredness that most people her age—nineteen—did not. Courtney's parents did corporate coaching, and she, an only child, had grown up calling them by their first names. She worked part-time for the family business and picked up a few shifts at Delilah's when she wasn't needed by them. Her parents would have preferred for Courtney to be enrolled in business school, working toward an MBA, but she had no interest in any of that. Courtney's passions were fashion, film, and sleeping as little as possible.

"Yummy," Perry said, as she always did when Courtney was filling the ketchup bottles.

"You do know this stuff is basically corn syrup," Courtney said. "It's got almost as many carbs as the other cheap sludge we use to refill the maple syrup bottles."

"Shut your filthy mouth," Perry said. "You know the rules." She pointed to the sign that only Delilah's staff could see.

The sign read:

RULE 1: WE DON'T TALK ABOUT CARBS.

RULE 2: SEE RULE #1

LOVE, DELILAH

Courtney shrugged and went back to refilling ketchup.

Perry got the syrup bottles and started refilling them.

Courtney asked, "How was the weekend? I heard you really gave it to a few people on Sunday."

"They were asking for it," Perry said.

"Oh, no," Courtney said.

"It was fine. They loved it. I was magnificent."

"No. I mean *that*. Now you've done it." Courtney put down the jug of ketchup and frowned at her best friend. "One of your dreadlocks is hanging in the maple syrup."

"First of all, there's no maple in this syrup. Second of all, that's how I like it." Perry lifted her long, medium-brown dreadlock out of the syrup and stuck the end in her mouth. "Delicious."

"You need to cut those off," Courtney said. "If you don't dry them out properly between showers, and I know you don't, they can grow mold inside. You're probably poisoning yourself right now with toxic mold, along with all the refined sugar."

"I like my dreads. They're a part of me. How dare you imply that they're moldy? It's borderline racist of you."

"You're white," Courtney said. "And I don't have an issue with dreadlocks in general. I'm just tired of getting whipped in the face by them. Plus I think you'd look so good with a cut like this." Courtney got out her phone and showed Perry a photo of a young woman with straight, shaggy layers.

"That girl looks boring," Perry said.

"She probably has a boyfriend," Courtney said. "Don't you want a boyfriend?"

"Ew." Perry grimaced.

The door chimed as the first customer of the day walked in.

Courtney saw who it was then jumped up and down excitedly. She grabbed Perry's arm and whispered, "There he is. Your future boyfriend. I'll finish the syrup bottles. You go take his order."

Perry wrinkled her nose. "Crossword Guy? No, thank you. He's so rude."

"You should try being nice to him."

"Why? I work here so I don't have to be nice to guys like him." Perry grabbed the coffee carafe and left her friend with the ketchup and syrup bottles.

Crossword Guy sat in his usual table by the window, like he did every Monday morning.

While Perry filled his coffee cup, he ignored her and opened his newspaper to the crossword puzzle.

Perry put her free hand on her hip. "Well? What do you want?"

"The usual," he said.

"Do you think you tip well enough that I'd be inclined to memorize your usual order?"

"Yup." He kept his eyes down as he filled in the first word on the puzzle.

"That'll be one very boring order of the basic breakfast, whole wheat toast, eggs hard-poached, and crispy bacon."

"You got it," he said, not looking up. "Thanks."

Perry might have given Crossword Guy some extra sass for his rudeness, but there was nobody else

around to witness it, and high-quality banter would
have been wasted on him.

Chapter 3

After a full shift on Monday, Perry Langtree walked home, getting thoroughly soaked by the drizzling rain.

At the Langtree house, she hung her damp clothes by the heater vent then started reading the notes her mother had left before going out of town. It was more of an instructional manual than notes. Mrs. Langtree had used a binder. With divider tabs.

Perry checked that day's meal instructions and took out the corresponding recipe card for spaghetti sauce. Her father, Mr. Langtree, loved mushrooms, and her brother loved zucchini. Mrs. Langtree had given her express permission to omit the usual carrots, as she wouldn't be there and she knew the rest of the family hated them in the sauce.

Perry's mother wouldn't be around for dinner for five whole weeks.

Perry thought she would be fine, but five weeks suddenly felt like a terribly long time. Perry pulled the carrots from the fridge and chopped them for the sauce as a form of protest.

That night at dinner, Perry's father and brother didn't say a word about the carrots. They were smart enough to not insult the person who would be cooking for them for the next five weeks.

Not about the food, anyway.

Perry's father leaned over her, sniffed her head, and said, "You smell like a wet dog."

"It was raining today," she said.

Perry's younger brother, a teenager of fifteen with the conversational maturity of an eight-year-old, said, "Perry always smells like wet dog."

Perry sniffed a dreadlock. The smell wasn't great, but she kept a poker face.

She stuck out her tongue at her brother and said, "If I cut them off, what would you bug me about?"

Garnet, the brother, grinned. "I'd think of something."

The kids' mother's name was Jade. She'd kept with the gemstone theme and named her children Garnet and Peridot. Peridot went by Perry, but nobody had ever come up with a good nickname for Garnet. The obvious choice was Gary, but Garnet wasn't a Gary at all.

"Maybe I *will* cut my hair," Perry said. "Just to keep you on your toes. Maybe I'll cut it right now." She picked up the knife she'd been using for the garlic butter and sawed at one dreadlock. The knife was sharper than she'd expected. A four-inch section of dreadlock fell away with no effort. The sawed-off chunk of hair, which resembled a caterpillar, landed in the butter.

Garnet squealed and stabbed it with a fork, forcing the fuzzy caterpillar of tangled hair deeper into the butter.

The two siblings fought over the butter and the hair. Things escalated quickly.

Mr. Langtree, whose name was Dale, which was not a gemstone, stepped into the sibling fight, muttering about how they were far too old to be acting that way. He halted the fun before Perry could get the buttery, fuzzy caterpillar of hair fully into her little brother's mouth.

Everyone returned to their assigned seats.

"Now you're lopsided," Garnet said, his eyes and tone mocking. "You'll have to cut all the others."

"Maybe I will," Perry said.

Dale said, in a calm, fatherly tone, "Your mother asked us all to not make any big decisions while she's out of town. Perry, I respect your personal choices, but I think you should wait until she gets back."

"Five weeks is forever," Perry said. She picked up the butter knife and unceremoniously sawed another two inches off the dreadlock. Then she dipped it in the butter and returned to torturing her brother, but it wasn't as much fun as it had been the first time.

Dale didn't even bother trying to stop the kids. He was busy arranging his cut spaghetti into a three-by-three grid on his plate.

The gemstone-themed siblings settled down again. There was no point to sibling rivalry if nobody was going to object.

"Dad, look at me." Perry snapped her fingers in front of her father's face. "Should I lose the dreadlocks? Be honest. Don't give me one of your dad answers."

He scooped a portion of food into his mouth and looked at her intently, like she was one of his diagrams of water pipes for his job at the city's Department of Engineering.

"It's your choice," he said. "Isn't it considered cultural appropriation for white people to have dreadlocks?"

"I'm not having that conversation with you again."

"Okay," he said. "But let me ask you a question. If it's not for cultural reasons, what purpose do they serve?"

"Balance," she said. "Big hair makes the rest of me look skinnier."

He said, "You're perfect exactly how you are."

"Perfectly stinky, like a wet dog," Garnet said.

"Thanks a lot," Perry said with sarcasm. "You two have been really supportive. Mom will be relieved I'm in such good hands."

"We're not supposed to be taking care of you," Garnet said. "You're taking care of us. You're the mother while Mom's gone. That was the deal."

Perry wailed, "Dad!"

Her father shrugged. "Your brother's not wrong. You're the one who wanted to have a year off before college. This was the deal you cut with Mom. You made your bed, now lie in it." He rearranged his spaghetti. "Speaking of beds and linens, I'm nearly out of dress shirts, so you'd better get a load or two of laundry started tonight."

In his brattiest voice, Garnet said, "Ha ha! You have to wash our dirty underwear!"

Perry said, "I hate my life."

Her father said, "Once you get into the swing of things, it won't be so bad."

Perry picked up the knife and chopped off another section of hair.

Chapter 4

Perry Langtree walked in the back door of Delilah's, exactly as she'd done about a hundred times already.

The cook, who was prepping hash browns, glanced up and said, "You can't use that door."

Perry replied, "Try and stop me, Hamster Biceps."

The cook's name was Donny, not Hamster Biceps. That was Perry's pet name for him.

Donny looked up from the hash browns and did an honest-to-goodness double-take. He looked at Perry, looked away, then his head went BOING. He looked back at her, mouth open and everything. It was priceless.

"No way," he said. "Girl, you clean up good."

Toph, the skinny young prep cook, walked out of the walk-in cooler, carrying a box of lettuce. He saw Perry and dropped the lettuce.

"Lipstick!" Toph pointed a finger at Perry. "You're wearing lipstick. And you have hair."

Perry checked her lipstick in the mirror above the dishwasher station. It hadn't smudged on the walk in, even though she'd touched it repeatedly.

"I'm trying out one of my grandma's products," Perry said.

Toph said, "And one of her wigs." He came over and tugged a piece of her hair.

"Ouch," Perry said. "It's real, you freak. Don't touch it again. My scalp is tender. It took me seven hours and a whole bottle of conditioner to comb it out."

"I like it," Toph said.

"Nobody cares what you like," Perry said.

Toph recoiled as though stung.

When Perry saw the hurt look on his face, she said, "Sorry. I didn't get much sleep last night. I only had one side combed out at midnight."

Toph started picking up the lettuce he'd dropped.

Perry turned to Donny and said, "You're a guy."

"Was it the sideburns that tipped you off?" Donny was in his forties and married to a professional potter. They didn't have kids, but they did have four dogs in various sizes, including a new puppy.

"Do you like the new look?" Perry fluffed her hair, which felt incredibly fluffy and different after years of wearing dreadlocks. "Would you want me to be your girlfriend?"

"Perry, I'm old enough to be your father." He threw some bacon on the grill to pre-cook ahead of the rush. "You look nice," he said. "If you were my daughter, I'd tell you that."

"If I were your daughter, would you teach me how to flirt and make guys chase after me? I asked my dad, but he's no help at all."

"Go figure."

"Lay your wisdom upon me, Great Married One."

"First of all, don't bother flirting or playing games." Donny pointed to his custom-designed black-and-titanium wedding band. "If you're interested in a guy, just tell him you like him. Or grab his face and kiss him."

"Without consent? Tsk tsk."

Donny shrugged. "That's what my wife did, and it worked."

"But you're *so* old," Perry said. She turned to the prep cook. "Hey, Toph. In your twisted little fantasies, when a girl flirts with you, what does she do?"

"She asks to see my pajamas," Toph said, referencing the conversation they'd had on Sunday, and the detail Perry had prayed he would forget.

"Thanks for nothing," she said.

As she walked away, she heard Donny asking Toph about the pajamas comment. Soon everyone would know. Oh, well. Secrets didn't last long in the Langtree family.

Perry checked over the dining room before unlocking the door.

Because it was Tuesday, Perry would be working the whole dining area by herself until lunch.

She got busy rolling napkins around silverware so she didn't get caught in a pinch when things got busy.

Half an hour later, even with her back to the door, Perry sensed her first customer of the day. She wasn't psychic, though it had felt that way until she'd figured it out. A human's body passing in front of the restaurant's doorway absorbed both street noise and sunlight—not dramatically, but enough that she could always sense when they were about to get the first customer of the day.

The first customer of the day was Crossword Guy. He didn't typically come in on Tuesdays, but there he was. He took his usual seat by the window and started unfolding his newspaper.

Perry walked over and filled his coffee cup.

Perhaps it was the Lana Langtree signature lipstick on her lips, or perhaps it was the lightness she felt—her head was an actual pound lighter—but something caused Perry to act differently that Tuesday morning.

Rather than gruffly demand to know what Crossword Guy wanted, she smiled and said, "Hello. Welcome to Delilah's."

He dropped his pen and looked up at her. He stared right into her eyes. His dark-framed glasses were on the table in front of him, so Perry had an unobstructed view of his eyes. They were a calming shade of blue. And, for some reason, they made her think about the weather.

Crossword Guy had nice eyes! The rest of his face wasn't bad, either. It was easier to see when he had his glasses off, and when he wasn't being his usual cranky self.

"Hello," he said back, just as warmly.

"We covered that already," she said impatiently, slipping back into her regular personality. "Try to keep up. What do you want?"

He blinked rapidly. "What's the special today?"

Was he serious? She recited Donny's special for the day: eggs benny with fresh spinach and turkey bacon.

Why did he want to hear about the specials? Crossword Guy always had the exact same thing. If Perry hadn't been distracted by his nice eyes and face, she might have resented him for wasting her time on the specials when they both knew he was going to order the basic breakfast.

To Perry's surprise, Crossword Guy said, "Spinach and turkey bacon sounds great. I'll have that."

So, they were playing a new game that morning. She could play along.

"Your wish is my command," she said in her robot voice. "I am the Waitress-Bot Three Thousand. I live to serve."

"Good one." Next, he did something Crossword Guy had never done before. He smiled. Perry had always assumed he was missing the crucial muscles to do so.

At that exact moment, the sun came out from behind a cloud. The nearly empty restaurant filled up with light and kindness.

Perry noted that Crossword Guy had a pleasant smile. He also had soft-looking brown hair with not too much hair product. Plus he smelled good. Like aftershave, but not the kind that older guys like Donny or Perry's dad used.

"Thanks," he said, still smiling, then he turned his gorgeous blue eyes downward and picked up his pen for the crossword puzzle.

In a daze, Perry meandered back to the pass-through window that opened to the kitchen.

"Sock it to me," Donny said, spatula in hand. "The usual?"

"Donny, I think I'm crushing on Crossword Guy."

"Are you on drugs? Either tell me what he wants or punch the order into the system." Donny leaned out to look up front. "He's the one who gets the hard-poached eggs, right?"

"No," she said. "Well, yes, but not today. He's having the special."

Donny shrugged. "I guess today is all about the surprises. First your new hairdo, now some sucker is ordering the special." The cook threw a pink slab of turkey "bacon" on the grill.

More customers came in, and the place started filling up.

As Perry worked, she could feel the pleasant sensation of Crossword Guy's gaze on her. While she took the next table's order, her consciousness left her body, and she saw herself from the perspective of an outside observer. It was disorienting. Her mouth got dry from nerves, like she was on stage performing in a school skit and she'd forgotten all her lines.

She was aware that Crossword Guy could hear everything she was saying. He was listening, and assessing her. Analyzing her. Trying to figure her out.

Dread washed over Perry. She liked attention, but only when she was putting on an act. Having someone watch the real Perry, the girl who just trying to do her job properly, felt like a violation.

The morning turned toward afternoon.

Crossword Guy lingered at his table, even though his crossword puzzle was finished. She thought about withholding coffee refills or threatening to charge him by the hour. Instead, she found herself smiling like an idiot and refilling his mug every time the level went down by more than an inch.

He looked up at her, the light from the window highlighting his great bone structure. "If you keep filling my coffee, I'll never leave and do my studying," he said. "If I didn't know better, I'd swear you were trying to keep me here all day."

She replied in a Southern drawl that matched her lipstick, "Maybe that's exactly what I'm tryin' to do, sugar."

He grinned and took a little more coffee.

After a half-dozen more partial refills, he finally left, slipping away while her back was turned.

He'd left the cash payment on the table. He'd left his usual tip, plus a colored postcard.

The postcard was for a local art show. She flipped it over.

On the back, written in Crossword Guy's tidy handwriting, was a note:

This is my friend's art show. You should drop by. -Marcus.

The art opening was that night at seven o'clock. There would be wine, according to the postcard.

Crossword Guy had a name, and it was Marcus. And he'd invited Perry to an art show.

The puzzle pieces fell into place.

He had been trying to drum up interest in his friend's gallery opening.

That explained everything!

No wonder he'd been so nice that day instead of his usual cranky, rude, annoying self.

Perry tossed the postcard in the garbage.

An hour later, she pulled the postcard out of the garbage.

Why not go? It wasn't far from her house, and there was a good place for french fries across the street. If the opening was boring, she could still salvage the night with fries.

Chapter 5

The art opening for Marcus's artist friend wasn't at one of the fancy galleries downtown. It was in the back of a restaurant that served Cuban food.

First of all, the art was bland. The paintings were swooshes of color on mostly-neutral backgrounds. It was the kind of art that looked fabulous in a photograph of a room, or in a condo sales center. Perry found one swirly mess that seemed to suggest a pair of big boobs. She stationed herself in front of it, looking around casually for Crossword Guy, also known as Marcus.

Marcus was standing with a group of silver-haired people. All of them were holding wine glasses and nodding in front of a five-foot-wide canvas with three stripes.

Marcus was also scanning the room. As his gaze swept across her casually, she felt it like a touch.

It was all suddenly too much for Perry.

She turned and headed for the door, only to be thwarted by a woman with a clipboard. The woman said, "I'll need to see some ID."

"Marcus invited me," Perry said.

"Who?"

"He's friends with the artist. But it doesn't matter because I'm leaving."

"If you don't show me any ID, you can't have the wine."

"Ew. I don't want wine."

The woman looked pointedly at the plastic goblet of sparkling white wine in Perry's hand.

Perry channeled the Langtree family charm. "This isn't apple cider? Oh, sugar, why didn't anyone warn me! No wonder it doesn't taste very sweet."

The woman sighed. "Drink it quickly and give me the cup."

Perry chugged back the wine and handed the plastic goblet to the woman.

As the woman left, Perry turned toward a painting so she could burp into her fist. She hadn't planned to drink the wine. She'd only taken a cup on her way in so she wouldn't look out of place.

A warmth spread over her body as the small serving of wine did its magic.

Perry relaxed into the feeling. The sounds around her became more pleasant. The gallery was pretty big for being at the back of a restaurant—over a thousand square feet—and quickly filling up with people, perfumes, and body heat.

From behind her, a deep male voice asked, "How do you like the painting?"

"I love it," she said. "And only a thousand dollars. What a deal. I'm buying this one for sure."

"You can't."

She whirled around to find the person attached to the deep voice. He was younger than she'd expected, around twenty. He had black hair, tightly curled, and big brown eyes. He had clear, dark skin, a wide nose, and a long face. He was very attractive.

Perry lifted her chin. "How would you know what I can or can't afford? I'm a fiscally responsible young person. I don't waste my money on avocado toast."

"Interesting. How is it that you're so responsible with your money when everyone else our age is broke?"

"I learned everything from my father, Dale. He works for the city. At his office, all they talk about on their lunch breaks is investments, the price of real estate, and what age they're going to retire."

"Dale sounds like my uncle. Do you put a portion of every paycheck into savings?"

"You bet your butt I do." She twitched her nose. "I'm not sure if that's the best strategy, though. My best friend, Courtney, spends every dollar she gets and then begs her parents for more. They always give it to her."

The tall, dark stranger leaned in. "Would Dale go for that?"

Perry giggled. Hearing a stranger call her father by his first name was exhilarating. "He spoils my brother, so probably."

"My family spoils my sister," the young man said.

"Every family's gotta have a brat," Perry said. "Now, who do I see about getting this magnificent piece of artwork packaged up and ready to drag out?"

He pointed to the red dot sticker on the card next to the painting. "You can't buy this painting because it's already been sold. That's what the red dots mean."

"Oh, I thought that meant the painting was Hindu," she joked.

He looked amused. "Actually, bindis are worn by women in other cultures as well. Muslim women in Bangladesh also wear the red dot."

Perry nodded as she admired the young man's good looks and overall wholesomeness. He could sell cereal. He could sell diet cereal.

He seemed to be waiting for a response from her, so she said, "What's the deal with the red dots, anyway? Who came up with that? Why not a sold sticker, like Realtors use for houses?"

"Things don't always make sense in the art world," he said. "The rules are different."

"I thought the beauty of art was that there are no rules. That's what my favorite art teacher taught me."

"There's art, and then there's the art *world*. Very different."

"You know a lot of stuff."

"I do." He held out his hand. "My name is Yaro."

Perry reached for his hand at the same moment a photographer stepped up and took a flash photo, blinding Perry. The photographer gave the young man a thumbs-up then moved on.

"Sorry about that," Perry said. "It's sort of a hazard of being in my family. Silly photographers."

"I think he was taking a picture of me."

Perry took a step back. "Oh, you're *that* Yaro," she said, connecting his name to the one on the postcard invitation and the signs everywhere. "You're Yaro Banks, and these are your paintings."

"I am, and they are."

She put her hand on her hip. "Do you always sneak up on people and trick them into insulting your art to your face?"

"You didn't insult my art," Yaro said. "The price has very little to do with the artistic merit of the art."

"How very well adjusted you sound. Are you sure you're an artist?"

"I am," he said. "And who might you be?"

"I'm a friend of Marcus's."

Yaro tipped back his tiny plastic cup of white wine, drinking half, then said, "Oh, I heard all about you. You're the funny waitress."

"I'm not just a waitress. I do other things. I can juggle, but only with three things, and they have to be soft." She leaned to the side to look around the wall that Yaro's body formed.

Across the gallery, Marcus was talking to an attractive dark-skinned girl with blue hair and multiple butterfly tattoos across her exposed back. She kept touching his arm and laughing.

"Who's the girl with the blue hair?" Perry asked.

"My sister, Sunshine."

"She's pretty."

"Do you want me to introduce you? Is she your type?"

"Hah. She looks like she'd be anyone's type."

"That's my sister."

"She's a lovely girl. Good genes must run in your family."

"What about your family? You look so familiar to me."

"I'm nobody," she said.

"That's not true. What's your name? I'm sure it's as beautiful as you."

"Peridot. Everyone calls me Perry."

"Why? Peridot is a beautiful name."

"I don't know why. That's just what people call me." She turned back to the canvas, which truly was growing on her. "I'm actually digging the art now," she said. "But don't get your hopes up, Yaro Banks. I'm not buying any, but I can appreciate what you're doing here."

"If you're not buying anything, I'd better go chat up some rich ladies who are."

"You should."

He continued to stand in front of her, grinning.

"Go make those sales," Perry said. "Make your uncle proud by being financially responsible." She grabbed Yaro by the elbows and rotated him to face the crowd of people who'd just walked in.

He turned his face toward her, ducking his chin to his shoulder, and said, "I'm nervous, Peridot. Keep pushing me. Be my coach. My wing person."

"Don't you have some sort of manager to be your wing person?"

"I'm on my own tonight. Can you help me out? You strike me as the type of person who's never at a loss for words. I get so tongue-tied when I'm talking to buyers."

"I can help you, but you probably won't like it."

"Let's find out."

She got close behind him then looped her arms under his armpits. She waved her hands in front of him like they were his. In a fake deep voice, she said, "Hello, art buyers. My name is Yaro Banks." She extended one hand in a mimed handshake. "What a firm handshake you have, sir. You might like my piece with the blue swish. You have a blue swish energy."

Yaro laughed. "That's uncanny. It's exactly what I sound like." He transferred his empty wine glass to Perry's left hand then tucked his hands in his pockets and pressed his arms down, gripping her arms firmly. She was stuck with him.

She waved her free hand at his face. "Careful what you wish for," she said in her imitation of his voice.

"How about I do my own voice, and you just do the hands?"

In her robot voice, she said, "I am the Arm-Bot Three Thousand. I live to sip wine from a box and shake hands."

"Perfect."

He walked both of them over to a gray-haired lady and said, "Hello. I'm Yaro Banks. Would you like to shake my brand-new robotic hand?"

The lady went along with it and shook Perry's hand like a champ. "No wonder your work shows such creativity and openness," she said. "You are a remarkable young man."

"It's the hands that should get all the credit for holding the brush," he said.

The gray-haired lady giggled. Perry had her face resting between Yaro's shoulder blades, so she couldn't see what was happening, but she imagined Yaro was putting on the charm. He did not need her help at all, the big fibber.

Yaro talked to three more people, interacting with them by creatively using Perry's arms.

He'd just finished the conversation with a couple of art collectors when someone tapped Perry on the shoulder.

She withdrew her arms from the artist's armpits and turned to see Marcus, formerly known as Crossword Guy. Marcus had the same wounded expression on his face he'd get whenever Donny didn't make his bacon crispy enough.

Marcus said, "I see Yaro has worked his magic on you already."

"Marc-o Polo," Yaro said joyfully. The two young men did a complicated handshake. Yaro was energetic while Marcus seemed to be going through the motions, one eye on Perry.

"Good turnout," Marcus said to his friend.

"Thank you for inviting this charming young lady," Yaro said. "We were just getting to know each other."

Marcus clenched his jaw. "From the looks of it, you two are best friends now."

Yaro patted Marcus on the shoulder. "I was only keeping her warm for you, bro."

"He was," Perry said. "Very warm. I was starting to sweat from all the hand shaking. Plus he's pretty toasty under that suit."

Dryly, Marcus said, "He always is."

Yaro said, "I'm going to leave you two to... whatever this is." He rubbed his hands. "I hope the gallery has a full sheet of little red stickers, because I feel very lucky tonight."

"Sell every last one," Perry said. "Be a superstar sellout." She swung her fist. "Go, team."

Yaro glanced guiltily at Marcus, let out one chuckle, then left. He made a beeline for the first lady he'd talked to, the one with the gray hair.

Marcus said to Perry, "I didn't think you'd come."

"Why would you invite me if you didn't think I'd come?"

"Maybe, deep down, I enjoy rejection."

"You are a weird dude, Crossword Guy."

He tilted his head to the side as he looked at her. "I feel like we know each other."

"You wish," she said.

"I don't even know your name." He glanced over at Yaro and frowned. "I'm sure Yaro has your name and your number."

"You have no idea," she said. "When I was pretending to be his hands, we went into the bathroom, and one thing led to another."

Marcus's jaw moved, but no sound came out.

"That's a joke," she said. "We just talked to some boring people about overpriced canvases with swooshes. I didn't put my hand in his pants. What kind of a girl do you take me for?"

"I don't know. I just met you today."

"I wouldn't say that," she said.

"Okay. Maybe we knew each other in a previous life." He relaxed and gave her a hint of a smile.

"What about your other girlfriend? Yaro's sister? The one with the blue hair and the butterfly tattoos?"

"She's not my girlfriend."

"But is that your type?" Perry held up one hand. "Don't answer that. It's a stupid question. She's gorgeous. I'm sure she's anyone's type. I'm not even into girls, but if she came up to me tonight and wanted to play Robot Hands, I'm not sure I'd say no."

"You'd like Sunshine," he said. "She's a fun person."

"But?"

"But I'm a fan of authenticity," he said. "Truth. Honesty. Not artifice."

"I'm down with authenticity."

"Says the girl with the false eyelashes," he said.

Perry had forgotten she was wearing full makeup and false eyelashes, courtesy of a hasty makeover at Courtney's house. Courtney would have come to the art opening, but she'd had other plans.

Perry touched the thick fringe on her eyelids self-consciously. They weren't so uncomfortable after all, once you got used to them.

She asked Marcus, "What's wrong with a little window dressing?"

"Nothing, I guess." He tugged at his shirt collar. He was wearing an actual tie, along with suit pants and a boring brown jacket that could have come from Perry's father's closet. Perry was used to seeing Crossword Guy in more casual clothes, like a T-shirt topped with a flannel shirt, but she liked him in a suit.

"You should have worn a blue tie," Perry said. "Or a blue shirt. To go with your eyes."

A smile played across his lips. "Maybe you can help me pick out my clothes for Yaro's next art opening." The smile rapidly disappeared. "If he can spare you and your arms."

"How long have you two been friends?"

Marcus frowned and looked up at the ceiling. "Fifteen years, at least."

"Did he start off ugly and awkward, and recently blossom into the fine young man we see before us?"

"No," Marcus said. "Yaro was always... Yaro."

"Then there's something wrong with you, Marc-o Polo. Can I call you that?"

"I'd rather you didn't. What do you mean there's something wrong with me?"

"You invited a funny and delightful young woman to an art opening for your best friend, who is a known charmer, and you get surprised when the two of them get along? I mean, come on. What did you expect?"

He looked down and ran a hand through his brown hair. "You didn't have to hug him for twenty minutes straight."

"You didn't have to watch me hug him for twenty minutes straight."

He jerked his head up, his eyes narrowed at her in suspicion. "I do know you," he said. "Where do I know you from?"

Perry didn't like the look he was giving her, or his tone.

"I'm out of here," she said. "This is too weird, even for me."

"What? I didn't do anything. You were the one who was all over my friend. Is it the money?"

Perry still had Yaro's drink her left hand. Her arm, seemingly of its own accord, jerked up. She was throwing a drink in his face, just like people did in the movies.

Fortunately—for Marcus, anyway—the plastic goblet was nearly empty. A single drop of wine flew from the glass. It landed, like a fat raindrop, in the middle of the right lens of his glasses.

Marcus gasped and took a step back. "It's you," he said. "You're always threatening to throw drinks at me, and you just did."

"That was an accident," she said. "My arm jerked."

He took off his glasses and squinted at her.

While Marcus was having a profound realization about who Perry was, Perry was not.

All she noticed was that there was a clear path between herself and the exit.

"It's been fun, but I have to work in the morning," Perry said. "I hope you and Yaro can work through your sexual tension, buy a nice townhouse together, and live happily ever after."

"A townhouse? What?"

"Good luck with whatever it is you two have going on. I don't want anything to do with it."

Just then, the photographer who'd blinded her at the beginning of the party reappeared. He raised his large camera with the big flash attachment.

Perry was ready that time. She squeezed her eyes tight as the flash went off.

Then, while Marcus was blindly blinking, she made her escape.

She grabbed three shrimp puffs on the way out.

Then she went across the street for french fries.

Chapter 6

Perry Langtree wasn't feeling very funny the day after the art opening.

She didn't let that stop her from doing her job. She walked up to the table of four and delivered one of her finest performances to date. It went a little something like this:

"Welcome to Delilah's, folks, where bad behavior is not just tolerated, but encouraged. If you want something and can't catch my attention, feel free to whistle. Someone will be out to change your diaper in a hot minute. The cook doesn't whistle because it's unhygienic, so he rings a bell like he's checking into a fleabag motel. I can start you with some coffee. If you don't like our coffee, which is dumped and fresh-brewed once a week, minimum, you can bring your own, but I'll warn you there is a dollar surcharge, a dollar twenty-five if it's Starbucks."

One of the bearded men, who had been there before, said, "I thought it was two-fifty for Starbucks cups."

"All your surcharges are double, sir, because you don't shave your neck. Beards are okay, but not neckbeards."

Mr. Neckbeard's friends all laughed and continued roasting him as Perry walked away.

More people came in the front door—singles for the bar, as well as some four-tops. Perry got busy seating, serving, and sassing, relieved the lunch rush was starting and she could lose herself in work.

Courtney was there, and the best friends worked in flow with each other, dancing and weaving between the diners, as graceful and entertaining as

Cirque du Soleil, except with airborne salt shakers instead of flaming sticks.

Some people practiced meditation to chill out and regain balance; Perry Langtree waitressed.

After the lunch rush ended, Perry put one last order in to the kitchen then parked the edge of her butt on the lower counter. The waitresses weren't supposed to congregate in the area, or sit on the counter, but they always did.

There was a feng shui to workplaces. Walk into any restaurant or retail store and see if you can spot the preferred hangout station for staff, usually behind the barrier of a counter. Feng shui consultants could probably be brought in to make sure restaurants didn't have any of those spaces, but the staff would be miserable and wouldn't stay long. A happy workforce needed a few rules they could bend. It was crucial to feeling valued.

While Donny grilled up the last lunch special of the day, he said, "Hey, Perry, how does your superpower work?"

Toph, who was supposed to be washing pots but was instead leaning on the salad station, chimed in, "Perry has a superpower?"

Donny explained, "She guesses how people like their eggs, and she's usually right on the money."

Toph asked, "Is it true? What am I?"

"You're scrambled, with fried onions and ketchup."

Toph frowned. "That's cheating. You've seen me eat that."

"I have seen you eat, Toph, and I wish I could bleach the sight out of my brain," she said.

Donny said, "Never mind the kid. How do you do it?"

"I don't know for sure. I just look at people, and my brain must compare them to all the people from the past. For example, skinny women with permed hair and wire-rimmed glasses like poached eggs. Once you know, you know. If I don't get a specific feeling, it's safe to guess over easy, since about sixty percent of people pick that."

"Sounds about right," Donny said. "I do more over easy than anything else."

He flipped the lunch order onto a plate, set it on the pass-through, and rang the bell.

"I'm right here," Perry said. "Why do you always do that?"

Donny shrugged. "My superpower is I never forget to ring the bell."

Toph laughed. "My superpower is..." He couldn't think of one, and the disappointment registered on his face.

Donny grabbed Toph in a headlock. "Don't worry, little squirt. We'll come up with something."

The two were wrestling as Perry walked away with the order.

Later, at the end of her shift, Perry was lingering by the front door, wiping down menus, when Courtney came by.

"You're done for the day," Courtney said. "Go home. If he comes in, I'll text you immediately."

Perry snorted. "Who? Crossword Guy? I don't care what he does. That dude has issues."

"You like him," Courtney said. "You want to steam up his nerdy glasses."

"I might have liked him, but it was only for a day. I've hated him for several months, and that's more important."

"You never hated him," Courtney said.

"I did. He was always so rude."

"He wasn't that bad. You only hated the fact that he didn't fawn over you the way the other customers do."

"How dare you!"

"Around here, people treat you like *you're* the rock star, and Crossword Guy saw right through the act. That's why, deep down, you always liked him. You only hated the fact that he didn't like you back."

Perry stared at her best friend. "What's my mom got to do with this?"

"I didn't say this was about your mom."

"You said that people around here treat me like *I'm* the rock star. How's that not about my mom? You know, Jade, the actual rock star?"

Perry's mother, Jade, really was a rock star. She'd met Dale Langtree when he'd been on the road with his mother, on one of Lana Langtree's international tours. Jade was known simply as Jade, no last name. Like Madonna, or Adele, or Usher.

"You need a lot of attention," Courtney said. "Not in a bad way. You know I love you, girl, but that thirst you've got for the spotlight can get the better of you."

Perry stared at her friend for a full minute then said, "I shouldn't have combed out my dreads. If I had them right now, I'd whip my head around really fast and whack you with them on purpose."

Courtney gasped. "That was always on purpose, wasn't it? I knew it."

"Maybe. Either way, you're wrong about Crossword Guy. I don't like him. I'm not even remotely interested. I might swap shifts with Maggie so I'm not here on Monday when he comes in."

"You won't."

"Watch me." Perry marched over to the work schedule and wrote a note for Maggie about switching shifts Monday. Then she put the note underneath some other papers, where it wouldn't be seen.

Chapter 7

Perry Langtree's family was not impressed with dinner. It was only dinner number four from Perry's mother's instruction binder, and things had taken a turn. The store had been out of their usual peanut sauce for the stir-fry, so Perry had made her own, using peanut butter and the other things she guessed might be in peanut sauce.

Garnet, Perry's black-haired, dark-eyed little brother, pushed his barely touched plate away. "I'm not gonna say it's the worst thing I ever ate, but if you added eggplant, it would be."

"Note to self," Perry said. "Add eggplant next time."

"Only if you want to kill me," Garnet said.

"I do what I can for the good of the family," Perry said.

Dale Langtree grabbed the salt shaker and gave his plate a liberal coat. "It's fine for tonight, Perry, but don't bother packing up the leftovers for me. I'll buy my lunch tomorrow."

"The store was out of peanut sauce. I had to improvise."

"You did? Excellent. I do applaud your effort and ingenuity."

Perry finished gnawing on her sickly sweet broccoli and swallowed. "I may have used too much ketchup," she said.

"There's no ketchup in peanut sauce," Dale said.

Garnet made a gagging sound and spat out some vegetables.

"You love ketchup," Perry said to her brother.

"There is ketchup in Pad Thai," Perry said. "What's the problem?"

"You are correct," Dale said. "Ketchup is in some sauces, which is why this stir-fry is not completely inedible." He took another bite then pushed his plate away. "I take it back. Sorry, sweetie. This is inedible."

"Oh, well," Perry said. "You can't win them all. My first three dinners were okay, right?"

Garnet said, "I miss Mom."

"The first three dinners were excellent," Dale said.

The three sat in silence a moment.

Perry changed the subject away from the food. "Dad, can I ask you something?"

"Sure," he said.

"Something personal?"

"I'm not giving you any flirting tips," he said, referring to the last time she'd asked him for advice.

"I will," Garnet said. "Keep your mouth shut and wear a push-up bra." He grabbed a loaf of bread from the kitchen and started slathering on butter.

Perry ignored her little brother and asked her father, "What does it mean when a guy says he's into girls who are authentic?"

Dale rubbed his chin. "Who said that? Are we talking about a specific guy?"

"There's a guy who comes in and does crosswords every Monday at Delilah's."

Garnet said, "He sounds like a winner. You should marry him."

Dale said, "In that case, you should be yourself, Peridot. Be your own lovely self. Like how you are with me and Garnet."

Garnet laughed hard, chunks of bread flying out of his mouth.

"You're so rude," Perry said to her little brother. "You're going to be sixteen soon, and you act like you're ten. Dad, I was way more mature than Garnet at that age, wasn't I?"

Dale declined to comment.

Garnet said, "Perry, the guys who say they want someone authentic don't mean it. It's just something they say to get ugly girls to sleep with them."

Dale gave his son a stern look.

"The stinky little troll might be onto something," Perry said. "Remember the first time Mom was a guest judge on the music show? All the judges told the contestants to be themselves and have fun with it. But that was just what they said for the cameras. What they actually wanted, according to Mom, was for the contestants to rehearse their butts off until they had every note and move in their muscle memory, then *pretend* they were having fun and being themselves."

"That is... more or less how the showbiz world works," Dale said. "And maybe the rest of the world, too."

"So, if I want to make a guy like me, I *shouldn't* be myself. I should figure out everything to say ahead of time and rehearse it."

"Not exactly," Dale said.

Garnet said, "Never mind that. Get the padded bra." When his father looked at him, the teenager said, "All's fair in love and war."

"My boobs aren't okay?" Perry looked down. "I thought I had nice boobs." She squished them together.

Dale smacked the palm of his hand on his forehead. "I know things are unusual with your mother gone, but is this really appropriate for a normal family dinner?"

"We're not babies," Garnet said. "And we're not a normal family. Our mother's all over the internet with half-naked rock stars."

Perry kicked her brother under the table. She'd seen the photos, and she'd tried to put the new ones out of her head.

Dale Langtree's face lost more color than it had when he'd first tasted the stir-fry.

"There are new ones, Dad," Garnet said.

"It's just promotion for the show," Perry quickly told her father. "So what if she posed with some music industry people? It's what they do. It's show business."

Dad got up from the table without a word and went to the fridge. "Don't you have homework, Garnet?"

"You're so lucky you're done with school," Garnet said to Perry. He grabbed two more slices of buttered bread and got up from his chair. "Homework sucks."

"Have fun while you still can," Perry told Garnet. "You don't realize it when you're there, but life's a lot simpler in high school."

"Yeah? If high school's so great, why don't people stay in it forever and ever?"

Dale pulled a beer from the fridge and cracked it open. "We do stay," he said, sounding weary. "We are all in high school, forever and ever. The pretty girls are always chasing the jocks, and guys like me are at the bottom of the heap."

Garnet gave his sister a wide-eyed look and then scurried out of the room. Both Langtree kids tried to avoid their father when he got into one of his poor-me moods.

"Dad, I'm sure it's nothing. You should call her."

Dale listened for Garnet's bedroom door to close, then he sat down across from Perry.

"You're eighteen," he said.

She didn't want to hear what was coming next, but it was too late to escape.

"You're practically an adult," he said. "I'm not going to sugarcoat it. Your mother and I aren't doing so well."

He took a long drink, swallowing half of his beer.

Perry's pulse rushed in her ears.

"Dad, did you take your pills today?"

"It's not your job to pester me about my pills."

"So, that's a *no* then."

"I forgot. I'll definitely take them tomorrow."

"Do you wanna watch a movie with me tonight? Let's relax. We can see how things look in the morning."

He drank more of the beer. "You don't have to look after me. That's your mother's job."

"Dad. Don't be like this. If there's something in your life you don't like, change it. You can change anything."

He shook his head. "Eighteen years old," he said. "At that age, I used to have hope, too. I believed things could get better."

"Things can get better."

He leaned forward, his elbows on the granite counter, and looked unwaveringly into her eyes. "Nobody grows up, and nobody ever changes."

Perry tensed her legs, shifting ahead on her chair so she could rub her big toe back and forth on the floor, searching for the gap in the floorboards. Once she found it, she jammed her toe into the gap. The pain in her toe would keep the other stuff from getting all the way in.

The rest of the evening was a write-off.

Later, after she'd climbed into bed, Perry sent her mother a full report.

Chapter 8

Thursday

Before leaving the house for work, Perry made sure her father took his medication.

They stood in the kitchen, and he made a big show about taking the pills, then showing his daughter his tongue. The back of his tongue was white and gross. He hadn't been using his tongue scraper. She'd work on that once the pills were taken care of.

"Sorry I was a downer last night," he said. "Your mother called around four in the morning. We talked."

"Good," she said. She didn't ask what they'd talked about. She turned quickly, causing the tassels of the scarf she was wearing to whip out and hit her father in the face.

"Watch it," he said, spitting a tassel out of his mouth. "Is that your mother's scarf?"

"Yeah." Perry had tied the scarf around her head as a hairband. "She said I could borrow some of her clothes. I like the feeling of the tassels swinging around and touching my back. It reminds me of my old dreadlocks."

He pulled a stray cotton thread off his tongue. "Getting whipped in the face reminds me of your old dreadlocks, too."

"If you don't like it, don't stand in the blast radius."

"I'll try not to," he said. "Have a nice day at work."

"Will do." She headed for the back door.

"One more thing," he said.

"What? Do we need more milk?"

"I'm proud of you," he said. "That's all. Peanut butter in the stir-fry sauce aside, you're doing a really good job filling in for your mother."

"Thanks." She opened the door quickly. Dale Langtree in one of his positive moods was in some ways more annoying than his bad moods.

He called after her, "We do need milk!"

"We always need milk," she grumbled, sounding exactly like her mother in that moment.

Perry walked to Delilah's with a bounce in her step, swinging her tassels.

When she got to work, Toph looked up from his half-peeled bowl of potatoes and said, "Nice scarf."

"Toph, are you flirting with me?" She flung off her jacket and posed like a calendar girl. "Do you really think you could handle all of this?"

He blushed at his potatoes.

Donny, who was oiling up his grill station, said, "Don't lord your unfair womanly advantage over the poor boy."

"What advantage is that, exactly? The ability to do more work for less pay?"

Donny shook his head.

Perry grabbed some blueberries from a nearby crate and sampled them for quality. "Seriously, though, how do I look today? Do I look *authentic*?" At the art opening, Marcus had said he was into girls who were authentic. Perry wasn't into Marcus, of course, but she was interested in becoming more authentic, whatever that meant.

Donny said, "You look really authentic with blueberry skins all over your teeth."

Perry asked, "Donny, what are your wife's best qualities?"

"That she doesn't ask me questions like that."

Toph laughed like a hyena. He always laughed at Donny's jokes.

"How about when you first met?" Perry munched more blueberries. "What did you like about her? What made her different from all the other girls?"

Donny shrugged. "She's the only one who liked me back. Plus she grabbed me by the face and kissed me."

"How romantic." Perry turned to Toph. "What about you?"

"I like girls who are rated a seven or better," Toph said.

"Really? But you're barely a six yourself, if I'm being generous."

Toph didn't disagree with the assessment.

Donny said, "If the kid here is a six, what am I?"

"You're also a six. That's still good. It's better than average."

"Then you're a six, too," Donny said.

"Six and a half," Toph said.

"Come on, guys. I'm at least an eight," she said.

"Courtney's an eight," Donny said. "That's why she always gets better tips than you."

Perry pouted. Courtney was several points more attractive than her, but it hurt to hear it from the guys.

Donny ducked his head to peek out the window-opening to the dining room. "You have a customer, Little Miss Six and a Half."

Perry said, "Call me that again and I'll tell Toph about how you had plantar warts on your hands and spread them to everyone in the kitchen via the utensils."

Toph threw the potato peeler on the floor and jumped back in alarm.

"They're cured now," Donny said to Toph. "Everyone who worked here had them burned off long before you got hired. You're safe."

Toph picked up the potato peeler gingerly.

Perry went out to wait on the first table of the morning.

It was two men in business suits. The man in the red tie was familiar-looking. He came in regularly, and he always fawned over Courtney, who was an eight, while Perry was only a six and a half. The world wasn't fair.

Red Tie was visibly disappointed to see Perry approaching the table with the menus. He actually glanced around, looking for Courtney.

His friend, Yellow Tie, didn't even look at the menu before asking Perry, "What would you recommend?"

"The place across the street," she said.

Yellow Tie gave her a confused look. "I meant from the menu."

"French toast with blueberries," she said flatly.

"That sounds terrific," he said. In a patronizing tone, he added, "Now, was that so difficult?"

"I just remembered. We're out of blueberries." They were not out of blueberries. She still had some stuck between her front teeth.

"Can I get strawberries instead?"

"It's extra," she said. It wasn't.

She finished taking their order and walked over to punch it into the system.

The music was low, so Perry could hear Yellow Tie say to his friend, "You told me the waitresses here were cute and funny. This one's just mean."

The friend said, "My favorite is the Asian girl. Just my luck she's not working when I bring someone new in."

Perry died a little inside.

Thanks to those comments, the two businessmen's dining experience did not improve.

Perry's day, however, did improve an hour later when an interesting customer walked in.

It was Yaro Banks, the artist who was friends with Marcus.

At last, a customer she could have some fun with. Not like the humorless office drones who'd been coming in all morning.

Yaro was on his own. Judging by the paperback novel in his hand, he wouldn't be meeting anyone. He had also brought in a takeout coffee.

"Mr. Banks, you are a naughty boy," she said. "Is that a competitor's coffee in your hand?"

He beamed a radiant smile at her. Yaro was tall, with a lean build. His long face and wide nose might have made him unattractive if they'd been slightly longer and wider, but paired with his clear skin and his big brown eyes, he was at least a seven. When he smiled, he shot up to an eight and a half. *Must be nice*, she thought.

He lifted his paper cup. "I paid six bucks for this at Starbucks, and I didn't want to waste it."

"You're going to pay seven twenty-five in the end, when I add your takeout cup surcharge."

"Totally worth it." He scanned the eclectic artwork on the walls. "I've never been here before, but I hear the coffee is the worst in the city. What exactly is the secret?"

"We toss the new grounds on top of the old ones," she said, which wasn't true at all. Delilah's coffee was decent for a diner, but everyone liked to play it up for laughs.

"Do you add banana peels, too? I think I heard that rumor about this place."

"Only on Fridays. And it's Thursday, so you might be safe."

"My lucky day," he said.

She handed him a menu. "These laminated rectangles contain words about food."

"No need to look. I'll have the clubhouse."

"How do you know we have a clubhouse sandwich? We might not."

Still grinning, he said, "All diners have a clubhouse." He leaned back casually in his chair. "Don't you have a little message pad you should be using to write this down?"

"Only if I care about getting your order right."

He grinned. "You're fun. What time are you off work?"

From somewhere behind Perry, a guy said gruffly, "I think that's enough."

Perry turned to find Crossword Guy, Marcus, standing behind her and looking annoyed.

"Thank you, sir," Perry said to Marcus. "Thank you for helping an innocent young waitress fend off untoward advances from a lecherous customer."

"Not him," Marcus said, pointing at her. "You leave my friend alone, you monster."

Monster? Perry was rendered speechless by the insult, and its accuracy. Perry did feel a connection toward monsters, which was why she made hand-stitched monsters as a hobby in her free time. How had Marcus known?

Marcus took the chair across from his friend.

"You made it, man," Yaro said. He pushed aside his paperback and Starbucks coffee so the guys could do their elaborate handshake across the table.

"Get a room," Perry said.

Without looking up, Marcus said, "I'll have the usual."

"We're out of that," Perry said.

He looked up, squinting at her through his thick-framed glasses. "You're out of bacon, eggs, and toast?"

"Strange but true. The last of the toast will be used for your friend's clubhouse."

Marcus narrowed his eyes at her. She narrowed her eyes right back.

"Then I suppose I'll have the chicken and grilled vegetable wrap," he said.

"It's got green, red, and yellow peppers in it," Perry said. "Are you sure you want to mess around with acid reflux today?"

His narrowed eyes went round, and he tilted his head back in surprise. "How do you know I get acid reflux from peppers?"

Perry hadn't known until she'd guessed and he'd confirmed it. She'd only guessed because it was relatively common, and it had popped into her head. Her father had acid reflux, and there was something about Marcus that reminded her of Dale Langtree, though she hadn't realized it yet. It was his particular combination of neuroticism and friendliness. She'd seen it in the way Marcus had reacted to Perry playing the role of Yaro's hands. His poor-me attitude had been similar to the way Dale Langtree reacted whenever Jade interacted with any man who wasn't him.

Perry, however, hadn't figured that whole thing out. She was only eighteen, and she'd never even kissed a boy, let alone dated one. There was so much she didn't know about relationships, people, or herself.

"Doesn't matter," Marcus said. "Give me the wrap. Put extra peppers in it if you want. I can handle whatever you dish out."

Yaro interrupted to say, "Bro, that's not how you talk to a girl."

"She's not a girl," Marcus said. "She's our waitress."

"Ouch," Perry said.

Yaro looked up and sweetly said, "I hereby apologize on behalf of my friend. He's having a rough day. He's not normally like this."

Perry turned to Yaro and momentarily lost herself in his big brown eyes. She was so glad he'd come in that day. Rather than feel bad about how lousy things had gotten with Crossword Guy, she would focus on Yaro, her new friend that she actually liked.

"We all have our bad days," Perry said to Yaro, smiling.

Yaro said, "How could a girl as pretty as you ever have a bad day? If I were you, all I'd have to do is look in a mirror, and it would cheer me right up." He leaned back and looked her over in a respectful way. "I like the scarf. It shows a bit of your personality. I'd love to paint you sometime."

Marcus made a strangled sound.

Perry fluttered one hand to her chest. "Me? You'd paint me? I thought you only painted swooshes and dots?"

"I do realism as well."

"I'm a fan of realism," Perry said. She narrowed her eyes at Marcus. "And authenticity."

Yaro nodded. "I can tell that about you. You may be one of the most authentic people I've ever met."

Marcus cleared his throat. "Any chance you can put in our order before the restaurant runs out of everything?"

"Yes, sir, Mr. Grumpypants." She winked at Yaro then left to put in the order.

She punched in Marcus's order as his usual breakfast instead of the chicken wrap she'd made him order. He was a jerk, but nobody deserved acid reflux.

Later, when she brought it to him, she would tell him as much.

Yaro Banks would laugh and laugh at his friend's expense.

Chapter 9

Monday

Crossword Guy showed up at Delilah's on Monday, his usual day, at the usual time.

"You deal with him," Perry said to Courtney.

When Marcus had come in on Thursday with his friend Yaro, Perry had enjoyed a bit of fun at Marcus's expense. But Yaro had been there. It was always easy to perform for a friendly audience. Marcus was there alone today, so the prospect of serving him didn't seem very fun.

Courtney went over, talked to him for a few minutes, then came back and said to Perry, "He wants you."

"He can't have me."

"He's in your section. I can't be running back and forth when it gets busy. Do you want to trade sections?"

"And have my entire day ruined? No way." Perry tightened the bow on her apron. "If Crossword Guy wants me, he's going to get me. All of me."

Courtney caught her friend with one arm and held her back. "He is a paying customer," she said. "Might I remind you that Delilah's is a business. It's not one of your mom's or your grandma's concerts. Why are you here, anyway? I thought you were going to switch shifts with Maggie."

"She didn't want to switch." Perry omitted the fact she'd pulled down the note asking Maggie to switch. What business was it of Courtney's? Perry liked working Mondays.

Courtney released Perry's arm. "Be nice."

"He invited me to his friend's art show, then he got snippy when I talked to the artist. I haven't seen petty jealousy like that since we were in the seventh grade and tried to be friends with Patrick Loh. Who needs that? He's got issues, Courtney."

"We've all got issues."

"Exactly. My dad's having another midlife crisis, and my brother is... well, you know Garnet. I don't need Crossword Guy's issues, too."

"But he is cute. He reminds me of the weatherman. The dreamy one. Lance Philby."

"I suppose he *does* have nice eyes, even if his glasses are boring."

"Be nice," Courtney said again.

Perry grabbed the coffee pot and walked up to the window table wearing her nicest smile. She was baring most of her teeth, anyway.

Marcus picked up a bouquet of flowers that had been lying on the table and held them up to Perry.

"Now what?" She filled his coffee cup, splashing the saucer. "You want vase service? You want me to bring over one of our two precious water pitchers so your flowers don't wilt? I don't even know what we charge for that. How about ten dollars?"

"They're for you," Marcus said, avoiding her eyes.

"Why?"

"To apologize."

"Flowers don't apologize, Marcus. People do."

He looked up at her with those attractive blue eyes and gave her a sheepish smile.

"That's what I'm trying to do," he said.

"Okay," she said, her tone softening. Marcus was petty and jealous, but back in seventh grade, Patrick Loh had never given Perry flowers. Flowers might have changed everything.

"You can do whatever you want with them," he said. "I should have gotten the vase so it didn't put a strain on your finite water pitcher resources."

"It's fine." She took the flowers and walked away in search of a container.

Donny, Toph, and Courtney all took a sudden interest in the flowers and buzzed around like a bunch of busy bees.

All four of them huddled in the kitchen.

Courtney said, "He likes you."

"These are legit flowers," Donny said. "They're from Gardenia, up the block. This isn't some cheap bundle of leftovers you get from the Quick Stop bargain bucket."

Toph stared at Donny. "There are different kinds of flowers?"

"Oh, son," Donny said, ruffling Toph's hair. "I have so much to teach you about the ways of the world."

Perry slapped Donny's hand away from Toph's head. "Wash that boy's hair oils off your hands and get back on your grill station, soldier. We have a paying customer, and he wants the usual."

Donny rolled his eyes and went over to the sink.

"I don't get it," Toph said to Perry. "You hated Crossword Guy last week, but you went to the art show anyway. He treated you bad that night, then he came in last week with his friend and insulted you. But today he spent some money on flowers, so now you like him?"

Donny said, "Very good, son." He looked upward as he dried his hands. "They grow up so fast."

"It's not like that," Perry said. "It's the thought that counts. It's the fact that he made the effort." She frowned and looked at Donny for answers. "Right?"

Donny said, "It's weird being the only grownup around here." He threw some bacon on the grill and turned up the radio that hung over his work station.

"He didn't insult me in front of his friend last week," Perry said. "He just called me a waitress."

The guys went back to work.

Perry hung back in the kitchen, watching to make sure Donny poached the eggs to the right level of yolk firmness.

She brought the order to Marcus, set it in front of him, and said, "So, what was getting you down on Thursday? Yaro said you were having a bad day."

"Did he?"

"It was either before or after you said I wasn't a girl because I was just a waitress."

Marcus winced. "You don't have to be nice to me and ask me about my bad day," Marcus said. "I don't deserve it."

"My grandma always says it's easy to be nice to people who deserve it. It takes a person with true character to be nice to everyone."

Marcus took off his glasses and looked up at her with blue eyes that were even bigger and dreamier without the glasses. "That sounds like that song by the country singer with the... tiny waist." He snapped his fingers. "Lana Langtree. You know what? That's who you remind me of. It's funny, but you look like a young version of her."

"That is funny," she said. "But it's also true, because—"

He cut her off. "I am sorry," he said. "I brought you the flowers because I have to tell you something. Promise you won't get mad?"

"I don't even care what you think, say, or do. Why would I care enough to get mad?"

He wound up and let it out in one exhale: "I didn't recognize you."

"You mean when I got to the art gallery? I did think it was rude when you left me standing there all by myself like some vagrant who'd wandered in for the free wine."

"No. I mean on Wednesday. I didn't think you were *you*."

"Is this about me not being authentic? I am authentic, Marcus. I may be a monster, but I'm also the most authentic person you'll ever meet."

He sighed. "I'm a creature of routine," he said. "It's pathetic, but when you're a loner like me, you stick to your routines. On Mondays, I come in here to get abused by the mouthy girl with the dreadlocks. On Tuesdays, I get a hot dog at the Quick Stop and chat with Justine."

"Are you trying to make me jealous? Who is this Justine person you've been talking to? And who eats hot dogs? Do you know what they put in those things?"

He grinned. He had a really nice grin. It was even better than his smile.

"My usual Wednesday thing fell through, so I came in here," he said. "I was a little disappointed to see that my favorite mouthy waitress with the dreadlocks wasn't here. It was a new girl, with straight brown hair. I liked my new waitress so much that I actually started to feel guilty about cheating on my Monday waitress. But I invited her to my friend's art show anyway."

If Perry had been holding something, she might have dropped it. "You came in on a different day and you thought I was an entirely different person? Just because my hair looked different?"

He winced and rubbed his cheek. "In my defense, I believe I had my glasses off on Wednesday. I'm quite nearsighted. Are you mad?"

"I don't know," she said. She really didn't know. "Do you want more coffee?"

"Yes."

"We'll deal with that first. Eat your breakfast before it gets cold. I made Donny wash his hands before he made it, so it's extra clean today."

Marcus started mashing the first poached egg onto a square of toast. Perry had seen him do this many times. After spreading the eggs evenly on the bread, he would break each slice of bacon into nine pieces and arrange them in a three-by-three grid on top. It was the sort of thing her father would do.

Perry got him a refill then waited on more customers as they came in.

Yellow Tie and Red Tie were back. They waited at the door, avoiding eye contact with Perry, until Courtney came by to seat them in her section.

Perry kept stopping by the kitchen to admire her apology flowers from Marcus. The arrangements that came from Gardenia Flowers were the finest in the city. Perry had never gotten flowers from a guy before—her dad didn't count—and the beautiful bouquet certainly set a high bar for future flowers.

Marcus finished eating, and Perry brought him his bill.

She said, "You didn't tell me what was getting you down last week."

"Boring stuff," he said.

"I'm sure it is. Tell me anyway."

"The usual. Career-choice woes, university dilemmas. I'm not sure if I'm on the right path. My dad wants me to intern at his place, and that might be more fun, but would I be trading short-term good times for a more secure future?"

"I wish I could help with that. As you can see by my comfortable shoes and apron, I won the lottery when I got this job. I know most people aren't as lucky in their careers."

"What I really need to do is interview a working engineer." He added, "Not the kind that drives a train."

"My dad's an engineer," she said. "Not the kind that drives a train."

"Are you serious?"

"He works for the city, on the pipes."

"Interesting," Marcus said. "It sure would be cool to pick his brain."

"He would love that. My dad loves talking about his work with people who care about engineering. He's kind of the odd one out in our family."

"Do you think he'd let me take him out for coffee some time?"

"Like a date? Shame on you, Marcus. My dad's married. And he's too old for you, anyway."

Marcus's cheeks flushed as he laughed. "Never mind. I'll ask around at the university."

"No. You may be onto something," she said. "If you promise not to come on too strong and steal him away from my mother, you can have access to him over dinner. I'd be there to supervise, of course."

"Sure. Do you want to meet here, or somewhere else?"

"Why don't you come to my house? Are you free tomorrow night?"

"Uh... I think so. You don't want me to come over to your house, do you?"

"Why? Is there something I should know? Are you not carpet trained?"

"Uh..."

She pulled the notepad from her apron and wrote down her address.

"I feed the animals at six-thirty," she said. "You can show up anytime after six."

"This is really nice of you," he said.

"Shh." She looked around the dining room. "Keep your voice down. I've got an image to maintain."

Chapter 10

That evening in the Langtree house, Perry announced that they would have a special guest for dinner the next day.

"I want you both on your best behavior," she said. "Dad, no moping about how hard it is to be married to a successful rock star who buys you anything you could ever want. Garnet, no embarrassing stories about me."

Garnet grinned maliciously and rubbed his hands. "What about that time we were camping and you peed your pants because you thought you saw a bear?"

"That one's fine," she said. "It demonstrates my solid survival instincts."

Dale said, "Why is this young man coming over?"

Garnet said, "Perry wants him to touch her body. Starting with the boobs."

Perry said to her father, "Not at the dinner table."

Dale put his face in his hands.

Garnet said, "My friend Kyle pushed the fat on his chest all the way up, and he put on his mom's bra. We all closed our eyes to find out what it would be like to feel a girl's boobs."

Dale kept his hands over his face and didn't comment.

Perry said, "And? How'd you like that?"

In a serious, thoughtful tone, Garnet said, "When I closed my eyes, I really tried to pretend it was a girl, but I knew it was Kyle. It felt like a butt. I didn't see what the fuss is about."

"You'll feel differently when it's a real girl," she said.

Garnet turned to their father. "Dad, how old were you when you touched your first boobs?"

"Older than you."

"Was it Mom? Was she the first girl?"

Dale kept his gaze down on his lasagne, which he'd cut into a grid for orderly eating.

Garnet squealed. "It was! It was!"

Perry gaped at her dad. "Really? There wasn't anyone before Mom?"

After a long moment, Dale started talking like he was narrating the movie version of his life. "I understand some parents have to confiscate all the phones and drive up to a remote cottage to drag honest conversation out of their teenaged children. How did I get to be so lucky?"

Chapter 11

Perry Langtree was concerned about Garnet ruining dinner, so she had the brilliant idea of inviting Garnet's friend Kyle to join them. Two fifteen-year-old boys were better than one because they'd keep each other occupied. Or so Perry figured.

Kyle was the boy who'd put on his mother's bra so his friends could feel boobs. Perry had a feeling the bra thing hadn't been Kyle's idea. Kyle was sweet and shy, with fluffy blond hair. He had a bad habit of picking his nose, but other than that, he was fun to have around.

The doorbell rang at six o'clock on the dot.

Dale looked at his daughter and said, "He's on time. I like him already. I shall offer him your hand in marriage."

Perry said, "Are you drunk already? Dad! You promised."

"I haven't had a drop. I'm as dry as a train station at ten in the morning."

Perry and her father were preparing veggie sticks. The two teen boys ran for the front door, fighting to get there first.

Perry heard Garnet greet Marcus formally. "Welcome to our home, sir. There's a bathroom on every floor. If you make a biohazard, you have to light a match."

Marcus replied, "We have the same rule in my house."

"It's for your farts," Garnet said.

Kyle giggled.

Perry yelled over her shoulder, "Let him in, you trolls!"

Marcus came into the kitchen with his shoulders in a high shrug. He was wearing a plaid shirt that was almost exactly the same as the one Dale was wearing.

He held out a bottle. "I brought this," he said.

Dale said sternly, "My daughter is only eighteen. How old are you?"

"Twenty-one, sir. And it's not alcohol. It's sparkling grape juice."

Dale let go of his stern expression.

"Marcus, Dale," Perry said. "Dale, Marcus."

Marcus offered his hand. "It's nice to meet you, Mr. Um..?"

"You can call me Mr. Um, or you can call me Dale. Your choice."

Marcus and Dale both grinned at the dumb joke.

Perry said, "Welcome to our humble abode."

Marcus glanced around. "It's a really nice house. Is it a new build or a renovation?"

Dale's chest puffed out. "It's over a hundred years old. We gutted it shortly after Perry's mother and I got married."

The two teenagers came running through the kitchen, grabbed some veggies loaded with dip, and ran out again.

Marcus said to Dale, "You have one girl and two boys?"

"God, no!" Perry's father practically shouted. "Not that we don't love the blond one. He's Kyle, and he's a good kid. If he asks you to smell his hands, don't. The other one with the jet-black hair, Garnet, is the fruit of my loins, along with Peridot."

Marcus raised his eyebrows. "Fruit?"

Perry rolled her eyes. "My dad's been using that term ever since the Paternity Incident, and none of us care for it."

Marcus wisely asked for no details about the Paternity Incident.

Dale said, "Do you like old houses, Marcus?"

"I love old houses," Marcus said.

"I'll take you on a tour."

As they walked away, Perry said, "I'll just stay here, slaving away over a hot stove!"

The microwave dinged.

Chapter 12

The teenaged boys finished dinner first and left the table, but not before an in-person demonstration of Kyle's ability to push his chest fat up to make boobs.

Dale Langtree and Marcus talked about school and career options. Marcus kept thanking Dale for being honest with him, and Dale kept saying it made him happy to put his knowledge and experience to some use.

As Perry was clearing away the dessert plates, Marcus said to Perry's father, "What do you mean you earn nothing? They must pay you good money these days. I don't mean to be rude, but houses in this area aren't cheap. I'm sure you do okay."

"What I earn is still nothing," Dale said.

Marcus furrowed his brow. "That's not the news I was hoping to hear."

Dale glanced at Perry then back at Marcus. "It's nothing compared to what my wife earns, let alone what my mother's got stashed away. Perry didn't tell you?"

Marcus gave Perry a wary look. "Didn't tell me what? Are you guys royalty or something?"

"In a manner of speaking," Dale said. "Music industry royalty. My mother is Lana Langtree, and I'm married to Jade. She's Perry's mom."

Marcus jumped off his chair. "No way! I knew you looked familiar!" He jabbed his finger at Perry. "I knew it!"

"You did not," she said. "You didn't even recognize me on a Wednesday as the same waitress who served you on Monday."

Marcus pushed his glasses up his nose. "Why are you working at Delilah's?"

"I have to work somewhere."

He shook his head. "No. I mean why aren't you a singer?"

"You would not ask that if you'd heard me sing."

Marcus made a sour face. "Since when does that have anything to do with having a hit song? Don't they autotune everyone these days? You've got the face, and you've got the pedigree. You're literally wasting money every minute you're not in a studio recording something."

Dale laughed loudly and cracked open a beer. It was his third one. Marcus had stuck to the sparkling cider.

"It's not what I want to do," Perry said.

"What do you want to do?"

Dale leaned in and echoed, "Yes, Perry. What *do* you want to do?"

"How should I know? I'm only eighteen. I've never even..."

They were both looking at her.

She looked at Marcus and confessed, "I've never even kissed a boy."

Marcus froze with his glass of sparkling cider an inch from his mouth.

Dale raised his beer bottle. "And on that note, I shall retire to my office to do some very important work."

Perry explained to Marcus, "He's going to shoot zombies. That's what he calls *very important work.*"

Dale called back over his shoulder, "Somebody has to save humanity after the apocalypse!"

Marcus managed to get the cider to his mouth and down his throat. His swallowing was loud.

"So, that was fun," Perry said. "I hope my dad answered all your engineering questions." She grabbed the remainder of the apple crumble and started licking the big spoon. "What do you want to know about growing up with a rock star for a mom and a country legend as a grandma?"

Marcus said nothing.

"Okay, then," she said. "How about you stare at me for the next hour and try to figure out what parts of my face resemble which famous family member."

"You have Jade's eyes," he said. "That's easy. I had a poster of her on my wall growing up."

"Who didn't," she said. "Did you ever look at my mom and, you know? Enjoy fantasies?"

Marcus looked away. Perry had her answer.

Marcus cleared his throat. "I should get going."

"Where? Do you have other plans?"

"I've got a lot of studying to do. Plus I've taken enough of your family's time for one day." Marcus put out his hand for a handshake. "Thanks for dinner, Perry."

Perry didn't shake his hand. "Stop trying to get away from my evil clutches."

"Your what?"

"Marcus, don't let all the stuff about my family being famous make this weird. Did you know I burned my thumb for you making that shepherd's pie?"

"Is your thumb okay?"

"Don't worry about my thumb. My point is, I wanted tonight to be fun for you."

"I did have fun. I'm glad your family is so interesting. I'm just a little... I don't know. In shock? Tonight has been an evening of revelations."

"We're just regular people. Don't let my mom and grandma mess with your head."

"It's not just that."

Perry understood what he meant, because it had been rolling around in her head since she'd blurted out her secret. The confession that she'd never been kissed. Rather than own it, she decided to fib. Fib hard.

Perry stuck her nose in the air. "If you're referring to what I said about never having kissed a boy, you should know that's just what I say in front of my family. My dad would flip out if he knew half the things I've done."

"So you have...?"

"I could write a memoir about my conquests," she said. A very slim memoir with one page and no text. "And then I could get that memoir published. It's one of the perks of being a celebrity's kid."

"I don't get this family at all," Marcus said. "Your dad is so normal. He's like my dad, except three degrees more normal."

"What does your dad do?"

"He's a weatherman."

"Your dad's on the news? Like on TV?"

"For twenty years now. When I was little, I thought everyone's parents worked on the TV."

"I get that," Perry said. "Whenever there was a big scandal about my mom, I'd get teased at school. I couldn't understand why the other kids never had to deal with their moms having a big scandal. What about your mom? Did she work on TV?"

"My mom's a local reporter. Well, she was. She works as a producer now, behind the scenes. She loves her job. It sounds like a lot of fun."

"We have a lot in common," Perry said. "You're a celebrity kid, too."

"Not like you. When I'm out with my dad, people will start talking to him like they know him, then realize they don't. But he's just a weatherman. Nobody asks for his autograph or gets excited about seeing him."

Perry said, "May I?" She reached across the table and removed Marcus's glasses. She gave him a good look then asked, "Is your father Lance Philby?"

"That's the one. How did you know? I don't think I told you my last name. What gave it away? Is it the eyes?"

"It sure is," Perry said. "Wow. You look exactly like your dad, except younger."

Marcus looked down at his hands. "That's what everyone says."

"Listen, don't worry about the sexy poster you had of my mom. We're basically even. I've had a crush on your dad since before I knew what crushes were."

"You did not."

"I did, I swear."

"You're just saying that to make me feel better."

"Maybe," she said. "Or maybe there's a shrine to Lance Philby and his dreamy blue eyes up in the attic. Who can say? You've got studying to do, and you're dying to escape my evil clutches, so we'll have to leave that mystery for another day."

Marcus put on his glasses and said, "Thanks again for dinner. Your dad was really helpful."

"I'll tell him you said that. He loves it when people find him helpful."

"I guess I'll see you at Delilah's."

"You might."

He edged toward the door. "I'm sorry you burned your thumb."

Chapter 13

Marcus walked into the Philby residence, hung his coat up, and went to visit his father. Lance Philby, the city's most popular weatherman, was typing on his laptop at the kitchen table.

Lance closed the lid and gave his son his full attention. "How did your meeting with the city engineer go?"

"Who?"

"Isn't that where you had dinner with tonight? Taco Tuesday wasn't nearly as much fun without you. Your mother accidentally bought the spicy salsa." He thumped his chest. "I'm going to have heartburn for days."

"You shouldn't have eaten it."

"Now you tell me. How was your dinner?"

"I met the engineer. His name is Dale Langtree. He gave me a lot of suggestions. He was way more honest than the teachers at school." Marcus helped himself to the leftover nacho chips that were still on the table from dinner.

"Langtree," Lance said, then he hummed a melody from one of Lana Langtree's hit songs.

"Here's the thing," Marcus said, crunching the nacho chips. "Dale is Lana Langtree's son."

Lance slammed his open palm on the table. "Shut the front door! You were at Lana Langtree's house? And you didn't invite me?"

"I didn't know. I only know Perry from Delilah's."

"What did I do to deserve such cold, cruel treatment? Your mother and I continue to let you live with us, rent-free, even though we are no longer legally obligated to. And you repay our kindness by hanging out with Lana Langtree without us?"

"She wasn't there," Marcus said, shaking his head at his father's over-the-top corniness. "It's not her house. She only visits a few times a year."

Lance Philby looked down at his closed laptop then suddenly looked up, his blue eyes bright and wide open.

"What about the girl? Pippa, or whatever her name is. You have my permission to marry her. I'll pay for everything."

Marcus crunched more chips. "I'm pretty sure that's *exactly* why she doesn't go around telling people who her family is."

"I'm only joking," Lance said.

"Like how people are always joking when they blame you for the bad weather?"

Lance frowned. "Well, that's just mean." He started crunching the chips as well. "Why am I eating these? I don't even like them." He took another and dipped the biggest one in the salsa. "Too spicy," he said, still eating it.

"Way too spicy," Marcus agreed, also eating the salsa that would keep him awake for hours that night.

Once the chips and salsa were entirely gone, Marcus said, "Her name is Perry, not Pippa. It's short for Peridot. The family has a gemstone theme. Her little brother's name is Garnet, and their mom's name is, well, you know."

"How would I know? I love Lana Langtree, but I'm not her number-one fan. I don't know her family tree."

"Her daughter-in-law is almost as famous as her."

"Nope. Never heard of her."

"Perry's mother is Jade. The singer." Marcus gave his father a duh stare. "Jade?"

"Oh," Lance said. Then he slammed his palm on the table. "Oh!"

"I know," Marcus said.

"Jade is that singer you had plastered all over your walls. You were obsessed with her. Don't you still have one or two posters up in your room?"

"Not for long," Marcus said. His fingers twitched. "I've got to take those down right away."

"Does this Perry girl look like her?"

"Dad." Marcus paused for drama. "You have no idea. She looks exactly like her, but younger."

"How much younger?"

"Here's the thing. I thought she was my age, but I found out tonight she's only eighteen. This time last year she was still in high school."

Lance made the *yikes* face.

"I know," Marcus said. "I felt like such a pervert."

"But you didn't do anything. This girl is the one who suggested you come over to her house and meet her father, right?"

"Well, yes, but I did initiate things by inviting her to Yaro's art show last week. You should have seen Yaro. He was all over her. He didn't care how young she was."

Lance rubbed his eyebrows. "Well, son. You're only twenty-one. It's hardly a scandal for you to be seen around town with a girl who's eighteen. However, it might be better if you waited until she was nineteen."

Something happened next. The weather inside the Philby house suddenly changed.

Lance's throat and stomach had been irritated by the hot salsa, and his words had come out sounding particularly caustic.

Worse, Marcus Philby's overclocked brain took his father's casual comments in the worst possible way. Marcus had been trying to sort out his future and figure out his life's path. He was making all the right moves, but he wasn't getting the answers he wanted. Nothing about Marcus's future was clear anymore, and his father was seemingly throwing even more problems at him.

"Unbelievable," Marcus said, pulling back in his chair. "Are you actually worried about how this might look *for you*? The fact that I like a girl might be a problem *for you*?"

"When one is in the public eye, one must always be mindful of optics."

"First you want me to marry her, and now you're banning me from seeing her? Thanks for the fatherly wisdom, Dad. Thanks a lot."

"I'm not banning you from seeing her. Do you think I fell out of a coconut tree yesterday? I know how reverse psychology works, Marcus."

Marcus clenched his fists. "Stop trying to manipulate me."

"Oh, grow up. I'm not going to indulge you if you're in one of your moods."

"I wasn't in a mood until you started lecturing me about how my life affected your precious public image."

"I was lecturing you? Are you drunk? On drugs?"

"No," Marcus said, practically growling. He noted, distantly, that he wasn't exactly on his game. Some chemicals in his system had changed recently. He had a new energy pumping in his veins that didn't feel good. Hearing Dale Langtree complain about the monotony of his career had not improved Marcus's general outlook.

Lance picked up his laptop and stood. "Do whatever you want, Marcus. You're an adult now. Make your own choices. Go ahead and turn down the internship I got you at the station. Make your own way in the world, like the stubborn donkey you are."

"Just because I stick to a decision doesn't make me a stubborn donkey."

"I don't know why you have to make everything difficult for yourself. Your mother and I don't understand you sometimes. If you didn't look exactly like us, I'd say the hospital mixed up a couple of babies."

"Just because I don't bat my eyelashes at everyone and use my looks to get everything I want doesn't mean there's anything wrong with me."

"It doesn't? Why do you think God gave you those eyelashes? You've got a finer pedigree than most kids your age. You should be at the gym working out five times a week instead of slouching around in those plaid shirts. And don't even get me started on the glasses."

"You're unbelievable," Marcus said. "How can they put you on TV every day when you're so wrong all the time?"

"I'm right far more than I'm wrong. Plus I have a fan club."

"Yes, you do." Marcus couldn't unclench his fists if he'd wanted to.

Lance snorted. "And that's a good thing, because I certainly don't get any respect in my own house."

With one more snort, Lance tucked his laptop under his armpit and left the room.

Chapter 14

Wednesday

Perry Langtree

Perry was thinking about Marcus when his friend Yaro walked into Delilah's.

It wasn't much of a coincidence, since she'd been thinking about Marcus all day. Dinner the night before had left her with so many questions. Why had Marcus been so eager to get away as soon as Perry's father had left the conversation? Was it something she'd said? Had the food upset his stomach? Was Marcus even interested in her as something other than a career contact? She had so many thoughts about Marcus Philby. What had it been like growing up with a popular weatherman for a father?

It would have been difficult for Yaro to walk in at a time Perry hadn't been thinking about Marcus.

"Hi there," she said cheerfully.

"If it isn't my better set of arms," Yaro said. "Shaking hands with people isn't the same using my own hands."

"Let's see," Perry said, extending her hand.

They shook hands. Yaro pumped her hand aggressively.

"You're right," Perry said. "My hands are a lot better." She glanced behind him. "Table for two?"

"Table for one," Yaro said. "My man, Marcus, isn't coming. Are you crushed?"

She lifted her nose in the air. "Why would I be? We serve plenty of singles. I'm not prejudiced, as long as you tip well and you don't stretch your legs out in the aisles." She waved the laminated menu.

"Right this way." She led him over to Marcus's favorite table.

"I'd rather sit at the bar," Yaro said.

"You want to watch the Flintstones? That's what we're playing on the TV today."

"That'll work," he said. "Plus I can watch you do your thing and bug you when you're not busy."

She led him to the bar, and he took a stool on the end. Perry walked around to the other side and rested her butt on the counter that the staff weren't supposed to sit on.

Yaro leaned way over and looked at the sign with the rules about staff not talking about carbs. He read it out loud. "Rule one, we don't talk about carbs. Rule two, see rule number one. Love, Delilah." He looked up at Perry. "Is Delilah a real person?"

"Once upon a time. She retired a long time ago. We like to pretend she's around. The cook, Donny, made that sign because he got sick of hearing about people's special diets."

"Speaking of which, what would you recommend?"

"The place across the street."

"Barring that."

"French toast with fruit."

"Sold," Yaro said, handing back the menu.

She put in the order and did some waitressing.

When she returned, Perry settled with her butt on the counter and asked, "Was there anything in particular you wanted to chat about?"

"What do you think of Marcus Philby?"

"He's nicer than I thought he was."

"I heard he went to your house last night," Yaro said, his tone teasing.

"You heard about that, huh?"

"I heard you made him a very nice dinner with no peppers."

"Did you hear that he couldn't get out of there fast enough once my dad left us alone together?"

"No, but that doesn't surprise me at all," Yaro said. "Marcus doesn't have a lot of experience with girls, let alone the ones who are as cute as you."

"You're quite the charmer," she said.

Yaro replied, "That's a good thing, because I am no painter."

"Don't say that. Your paintings are pretty good, considering they aren't paintings of anything in particular."

"They really are," he said, grinning widely. "I'm working on some large-scale pieces for a custom order. A commission. It's really coming together. It's probably my best work yet."

"It must be nice not getting insecure about your work," she said. "When my mom writes a new song, she paces around the house, talking about how terrible it is and how her best work is behind her. Then we all have to boost her back up by raving about how talented and luminous she is."

"Your mother, Jade," Yaro said.

"Is there anything Marcus didn't tell you?"

"He didn't explain to me why he left your house without getting a single kiss from you."

Perry looked down. Her cheeks felt hot. "It was late, and I think he had homework," she said.

The bell rang. It was the french toast. Perry grabbed it and tossed it in front of Yaro. "The fruit compote is excellent this week. When you're done, you'll probably want to lick the plate. Try to control yourself and at least wait until my back's turned."

Yaro laughed. He grabbed a fork and knife and cut a piece straight out of the middle of the stack. It was the exact opposite method of eating that Marcus would have used—or Perry's father, for that matter. Yaro truly was an artist, not an engineer.

"I've got an idea," Yaro said, munching on the breakfast. "How would you like me to coach you?"

"In art? I make some little monster creatures out of random bits of fabric and things, but it's not really art."

Yaro grinned. "You do? I'd love to see those sometime." He sipped his coffee. "What I meant was, how about I coach you on how to date Marcus Philby?"

"What?"

"You heard me. I know you like him. And I think he likes you. But this whole process could take a thousand years if you guys don't get some help along the way."

Perry crossed her arms. "Does he know you're here? Did he set you up to do this?"

Yaro rolled his eyes and pulled his head back. "Does that sound like something Marcus Philby would do?"

"I barely know the guy, but no. I guess not."

"What do you say? Can I be your Cupid?"

"What's the catch? You want a staff discount?"

"No catch," he said. "And the food here is already quite reasonably priced for the quality."

"They why would you want to help me?"

"Because I'm a friend looking out for another friend. One with very talented hands." He extended his hand. "Deal?"

Perry found the offer hard to resist. Yaro was such a charmer. If a proposal to eat kale salad had come from Yaro, she probably would have found it hard to resist.

"Deal," she said, and they shook on it. "Now what?"

"Tell me about yourself," he said. "Tell me about these monsters you've been making in your mad scientist lab."

"I can show you. We keep one here." She grabbed the frizzy-haired, button-eyed humanoid monster from the tub of crayons they kept around for kids. She tossed it on the counter between them. The elasticated joints inside caused it to wriggle as though alive.

Yaro's eyes bugged out, and he jumped backward off his stool in alarm. "What is that thing?"

Perry knew he was joking around, but his overreaction hit her funny bone hard. She started laughing and couldn't stop. She'd never laughed so hard at work, and that was saying something, because the staff was known for getting up to some pretty outrageous shenanigans. Earlier that morning, they'd filled Toph's nostrils with green peas and had a shoot-out.

That Wednesday, Yaro stayed for two hours and five coffee refills.

They talked about art, and music, and movies.

Somewhere in the middle of it all, they did manage to talk about Marcus Philby, for exactly forty-five seconds.

Chapter 15

Perry Langtree had barely walked in the back door of Delilah's for work that day when she got hit with a barrage of questions.

Donny and Toph wanted to know all about the guy who'd sat at the bar for "seventeen hours" the day before, flirting with Perry. He'd still been there when the kitchen shift switched over, so they hadn't gotten the scoop on Wednesday.

Perry said, "First of all, he was only here for two hours, not seventeen. Second of all, he's just a friend."

Donny rubbed his sideburns thoughtfully then twirled his wedding band. "Then why did you let him take Mitzi home?"

Toph said, "I don't get it. What's Mitzi? Is that a euphemism for something else?"

"Mitzi is the handmade doll I brought in. We keep her in the crayon bucket, for the kids."

Toph's eyes bugged. "You mean the Nightmare Witch? Why would anyone want that?"

"Yaro Banks is an artist," Perry said. "He wants to show it around to some friends at the gallery. He says they're always looking for up-and-coming artists to showcase."

"But you're not an artist," Toph said.

Donny said, "Like you'd know an artist if it bit you on the nose." He waved at the walk-in cooler. "How are those eggs I asked for coming along? Are you going to lay them yourself?"

"Yeah," Toph said, jerking his head back and forth like a chicken. "That's what I'm gonna do." He made his arms into wings and squatted. "Bok bok." His face went red with effort.

Donny said, "Listen, kid, whatever comes out of you, I don't want to know about, and I certainly don't want to touch it. When I took off my work clothes at home yesterday, I had green peas stuck in places they shouldn't be."

Toph stayed squatted and made more chicken noises.

The back door opened. Perry's best friend, Courtney Liu, entered. She looked at Toph, squatting like a chicken, then at Donny, who was attempting to groom his sideburns with a pair of tongs, and said, "I seriously need to reevaluate my career choices."

Courtney hung up her coat then said to Perry, "I heard you were flirting with a cute guy at the bar all day yesterday."

"How would you know? Is there a group text I'm not part of?"

Donny and Toph suddenly had things they needed to do. Donny started oiling the grill, and Toph ran into the cooler, muttering about eggs.

Perry put her hands on her hips and glared at her best friend. Her *supposed* best friend. "Is it a group text where you all make fun of me?"

Courtney said, "Of course not. We also make fun of Maggie and everyone else."

"Fair enough," Perry said. "I'm on a chain for making fun of you."

"I know," Courtney said. "Toph always forwards me the funniest highlights."

"I knew he was doing that," Perry said. She'd had a strong suspicion, anyway.

"Who was the guy?" Courtney asked. "Don't lie. Donny sent me a photo in the group text. I already know it was Yaro Banks, the artist who does the boring abstract paintings."

"That's who it was," Perry said. "He was here for only two hours. Not quite long enough for the food poisoning to kick in."

"That's good. We have a seating time limit for a reason," Courtney said, patting her asymmetrical straight black hair.

"He took Mitzi with him," Perry said. "He's going to talk to some gallery owners about me doing a show."

Courtney smirked. She grabbed a bag of napkins and walked out to the dining room to refill the dispensers.

Perry followed her out. "What's that smirk about? You don't think I could pull off an art show?"

"Are you kidding? I love your textile art. You've got more talent than half the kids whose parents pay the big bucks for art school." She pointed at her face and smirked again. "*This* is the face of someone who knows that Yaro Banks is going to be your boyfriend."

"Nope."

"Yup." Courtney reached for Perry's hands and jumped up and down. "Your first boyfriend! It's happening!" She squealed with excitement.

Perry didn't squeal or bounce up and down. She pulled her hands away from Courtney's.

"It's not like that," Perry said. "He's just my dating coach. He thinks I should be with Marcus."

"Crossword Guy? I thought you were back to hating him after he ran screaming from your house on Tuesday night. You don't hate him?"

"I don't think so. He didn't run away screaming. Actually, now that I think about it, he was more relaxed than most people would be after dining with two fifteen-year-olds, one of whom disappeared during dinner and reappeared wearing one of my sports bras stuffed with socks."

"Your brother put on your bra? I'd kill him."

"It was Kyle."

"That does sound like something Kyle would do. Sweet kid. We love Kyle. But he is Kyle."

"Oh, Garnet was definitely the mastermind behind it."

"Sounds about right."

"At least they only told one story about me peeing my pants."

"Dinner with your family can be intense," Courtney said. "Your dad always talks about pipes and the politics at his office, which nobody wants to hear about, but if you mother says one tiny thing about her career, your dad sulks."

"He does not," Perry said.

Courtney kept shoving napkins into the dispensers as she raised her eyebrows at her friend.

"You're right," Perry said with a sigh. "He does sulk. You'd think he'd be happier with her out of the house, but it's the opposite. I'll have to ask Marcus over for dinner again just so they can talk about pipes, and so I don't have to confiscate my dad's razor blades."

"That's not funny," Courtney said.

"And his long ties."

"Still not funny."

"You're telling me. I'm the one who lives with the guy."

The door chimed as the first customers of the day walked in.

The remainder of Thursday played out in the usual fashion, except for one thing.

The girls worked the same shift and split the restaurant evenly, as usual, but Perry ended up with more tips than Courtney.

"Stop gloating," Courtney said. "I must have given someone back too much change."

"I'm not gloating. I'm just glad I've levelled up to a nine. Do you think it's the lipstick? The eyeliner?" Perry batted her eyelashes.

"You're not wearing any makeup," Courtney said.

Perry remembered she'd rushed out of the house that morning and hadn't put on makeup. She hadn't done anything special to alter her appearance.

"What happened?" Perry asked. "Was I nicer to people today? Or funnier?"

"I don't know," Courtney said, frowning. "You have a different energy. Maybe it's because you went from having zero romantic prospects to having two guys after you."

Perry snorted. "Do not."

"Do too."

"Yaro is only coaching me to help me get Marcus."

"Keep telling yourself that."

Chapter 16

Perry and Courtney both had Saturday off together for a change.

The two girls sat on the front step of Perry's house, waiting for Yaro Banks to pick them up for the "surprise" he had been text messaging Perry about all day Friday.

Perry had a surprise of her own. Yaro didn't know it yet, but Courtney would be going with them.

Courtney had the crazy idea that Yaro was only pretending to be a dating coach so he could get through Perry's defenses and, in Courtney's words, "storm the castle."

The girls had been using various castle terms as metaphors for deeper levels of intimacy.

As they sat on the step, waiting for Yaro, Courtney said, "You need to put more alligators in the moat around your castle."

Perry swished her mouth from side to side. "Are we talking about chastity belts?"

"Metaphorically," Courtney said. "No matter what this Yaro Banks guy says, don't let down your drawbridge."

"I'm not even sure I'd know how," Perry said. "My drawbridge has been firmly shut since forever."

"You'll know how. It's instinctive."

"Easy for you to say. You've been having your castle stormed for years now."

"Excuse me? My castle is not exactly a tourist trap."

"It's not? Then why do you make everyone exit through the gift shop?"

Courtney scratched her head, ruffling her asymmetrical black bob. "Everybody loves a souvenir," she said. "Even if it's just a tacky fridge magnet."

"How many people have stormed your castle, anyway?"

"Only a couple of knights," she said. "Plus a few princesses."

"Must be nice to have a castle worthy of royal visits."

An enormous yellow Range Rover pulled up in front of the house.

Courtney asked, "Is that his? Is he rich? I thought he was supposed to be an artist."

Yaro jumped out of the driver's side and walked up to the house with his arms held out from his sides in apology. "It's my mom's car," he said, seemingly knowing what the girls had been talking about.

Perry introduced them. "This is my best friend in the whole world, Courtney Liu."

Yaro said to Courtney, "How should we settle this? I thought I was Perry's best friend."

"Ha ha," Courtney said. "Pace yourself with the charm. I'm coming with you two on your *friend date* today."

"Date?" Yaro feigned confusion, glancing behind himself.

Perry said, "Courtney's worried you might try to storm my castle if I don't have a chaperone."

"Okay," Yaro said. "That's what friends do for friends. They chaperone each other."

Courtney narrowed her eyes at him and said nothing.

Yaro pointed to the fishing tackle box on the front step. "Are those your creatures?"

"It's a dozen of them, like you asked for," Perry said. "Do you want to see them now?"

Courtney said, "They don't like bright daylight. They're creatures of the night."

Perry elbowed her friend.

Yaro leaned forward and held his hands over the tackle box. "I can feel them in there," he said. "There's a lot of energy radiating from these creatures. So many heartbeats. So many monsters crying out for love."

Perry said, "Now you're making me feel bad about shoving them in an old tackle box."

"My friend will have some ideas for displaying them," Yaro said. "May I load them into the truck? It's got an excellent security system, and I promise I'll safeguard them with my life."

"Load them up," Perry said.

While Yaro was opening the back of the yellow Range Rover, Courtney grabbed her best friend's arm. "I wouldn't trust that guy with a box of dog biscuits," she said.

"But he's so sweet and goofy."

"Exactly," Courtney said. "The worst thing is I actually like him already, which is a giant red flag, because I *never* like anyone when I first meet them."

It was true. Courtney was the first one who'd declared that Marcus, known then as Crossword Guy, was not a great customer. Perry had likely been influenced by her friend more than Marcus's actual behavior, which hadn't been at all bad on his first few Monday morning visits to Delilah's.

Perry said, "Why not go with it and let yourself like Yaro? You two would be adorable together."

"Maybe," Courtney said. "Nobody has trampled their horses over my drawbridge in a while. Plus it would keep him away from you."

"It's so noble of you to make sacrifices for your best friend."

"I do what I can. You've been good to me over the years, aside from this recent development of you earning higher tips than me."

"I'm sure things will return to their normal balance. They always do."

Yaro honked the horn of the Range Rover. He lowered the window and yelled out, "Are we doing this or not, ladies?"

The girls jumped into the vehicle. Both of them got in the back seat.

Yaro turned and grinned at them. "Is this how it's going to be? I'm your taxi driver?"

The girls nodded.

Yaro put the vehicle into drive. "Serves me right for telling my mother to get the yellow one."

Chapter 17

Perry Langtree, Courtney Liu, and Yaro Banks arrived at the secret destination.

It was the local community center.

Heads turned at the sight of the ostentatious bright-yellow vehicle. People didn't stare too long, though. Outlandish vehicles weren't that unusual for the neighborhood, which had an eclectic mix of housing at different prices.

Courtney started guessing what activity they would be doing that Saturday.

"Cooking classes," Courtney said.

"Nope," Yaro said.

"Tai Chi?"

"Nope."

"Introduction to Mandarin?"

"Nope."

"That's too bad. My parents would be thrilled if I took an interest in learning Mandarin."

"Don't let that stop you," Yaro said, chuckling.

"I'd rather learn German," Courtney said. "I like how hard it sounds. Can't you picture me yelling at people in German? It would be cute, right?"

"You're always cute," Perry said. "Yaro, isn't Courtney cute?"

"Cute as a button," he said, climbing out of the vehicle.

He came around and extended a hand to help both of the girls jump down, Courtney first, then Perry.

After Perry had reached the ground, he held on a bit longer than necessary. Perry thought about how many times she and Yaro had touched already. At the art show, she'd practically hugged him for an extended time. On Wednesday at Delilah's, they'd shaken hands at least twice, plus he'd also taught her the secret handshake he did with Marcus. Now he was basically holding her hand in the community center parking lot.

Perry chalked it up to Yaro Banks being a friendly, extraverted sort of guy.

He dropped her hand before she could think about it too much.

The three entered the community center. Yaro led the way down a hallway. He stopped by a closed door and knocked gently.

A woman's voice from inside yelled, "Come on in. It's unlocked, and nobody's naked!"

Yaro turned to Perry and Courtney, smiling.

Perry asked, "Why would someone be naked?"

He opened the door and nodded for them to follow him in.

The room must have been used as a daycare, among other things. It was full of toys, and all the tables were knee height with tiny chairs to match. The daycare stuff was all pushed to the edges of the room.

In the middle of the room, sitting on folding chairs in a circle, were about twenty people, ranging in ages from teens to retirees. All of them had easels holding big sheets of paper on spiral sketchbooks.

The eldest person, a man with white hair tied back with a piece of leather, looked right at Perry and made a sour expression. "Not enough curves," the man said. "I want voluptuous. I paid my twelve dollars. Nobody ever listens to me."

A woman with curly salt-and-pepper hair stood and offered Perry her hand. "I'm Gabrielle Banks," she said. "I'm the art teacher."

"Nice to meet you." Perry shook the woman's hand. Like Yaro, Gabrielle had dark skin, a long face, and a wide nose. Was she his older sister or his mother?

Gabrielle said to Perry, "You're a bit late, so let's get you disrobed right away. There's a screen you can use in the corner."

Perry blinked rapidly. What was happening? "Disrobed?"

Gabrielle Banks said, "We're not here to paint people in blue jeans, sweetie."

"Hang on now," Perry said, raising a finger and channeling her grandmother's sass. "I may be old-fashioned, but I think you should at least buy a girl a cup of coffee before you ask her to disrobe. Being naked in front of a bunch of strangers is not what I signed up for today."

"Sorry," the woman said. She turned to Courtney and shook her hand. "Cold hands," the art teacher commented. "You can go ahead and disrobe. I've turned up the thermostat, so the room should be warmer in a few minutes."

Courtney said, "Okay," and started toward the corner.

Perry grabbed her friend and yanked her back. Courtney could be *too* adventurous sometimes.

Yaro laughed. "Mom! They're not models," he said. "They're my friends. Perry here is the textile artist I was telling you about, and this is her friend, Courtney. Do you have room for a few more students?"

Gabrielle frowned.

The old man with the ponytail piped up, "Somebody had better get their clothes off soon. We're running out of time. I paid my twelve dollars." He continued to grumble, "Nobody listens to me. I keep saying we should meet half an hour earlier to get this chitchat out of the way."

Gabrielle sighed and said to Yaro, "Honey, would you mind stepping in? I don't think the new girl I booked for today is going to show."

"Sure, Mom," he said. "I can fill in." He turned to the girls. "That is, if it's okay with Perry and Courtney."

Courtney said, "You're going to disrobe, and then we're going to draw you?"

"That's how it works. You're not uncomfortable with the human form, are you?"

Courtney said, "As long as your human form stays several feet away and doesn't attempt to storm anyone's castle."

Yaro grinned. "I always behave myself when my mom's in the same room."

Gabrielle said, "Not always."

The old man who'd been complaining said, "Let's get this show on the road already. Let's see the beefcake."

Yaro's grin didn't falter. He said to the girls, "And this is *exactly* why I pose for free down here at the community center. The compliments from the eager students are all the pay I need."

Gabrielle set up two more easels and invited the girls to take a seat.

Yaro disappeared behind the folding screen.

Perry leaned over and whispered to Courtney, "I'm so glad you're here with me."

Courtney whispered back, "I feel like we should say something to honor this moment. It's your first time seeing a man naked in real life, isn't it?"

"I have a brother," Perry said. "Plus I've seen his friend Kyle naked countless times. That kid is way too comfortable with nudity."

"This isn't Kyle wandering around your house looking for a towel. This is a full-grown man."

Courtney picked up a charcoal pencil and made a tentative mark on the corner of her paper. "You don't think Yaro set this whole thing up, do you?"

"You heard his mom. They were expecting a woman, and she didn't show up."

"I don't know. The suspicious part of me thinks he wanted us to see him naked today. Or you, at least. Which is too bad, because I really like him."

"Why would he set this up? How is me seeing him naked supposed to get me closer to Marcus?"

"You are so naive. I'm surprised you have any castle left at all."

"Worry about your own castle and leave mine alone."

Courtney might have had more to say on the subject, but the model stepped out from behind the screen. He was wearing a robe.

Perry sighed with relief. She could handle a man in a robe, even if the robe revealed muscular thighs that made her feel funny. Not funny-ha-ha, but the other kind of funny. She would be okay, though. It was just legs.

Then Yaro stepped up on a platform in the center of the circle and dropped his robe.

Gabrielle Banks said to the group, "I'll just go over the nude sketching etiquette for the benefit of our two new students."

Perry and Courtney exchanged a look. There was etiquette?

The teacher said, "Do not touch, photograph, or talk to the model."

Perry and Courtney smirked at each other. That seemed obvious enough.

The teacher said, "Do not take off your own clothes."

Perry and Courtney giggled.

She said, "I only mention that because it has happened."

The old man who'd been grumbling said, "I was hot."

"Not you, Larry," Gabrielle Banks said. "It's fine to remove a cardigan or extra layer if you wish. The room is quite warm, for the comfort of the model. However, if you do remove a sweater, do not sing a striptease melody." She looked at Larry. "That one is aimed at you."

Larry ignored her. He was already sketching, his hands moving swiftly across the large sheet of paper.

Gabrielle Banks said, "The model will hold a series of poses for one minute each, while we do quick sketches to loosen up." She clapped her hands. "Quick, quick everyone, forty-five seconds remaining!"

Everyone else was already sketching the first pose. Perry's hands were sweaty. She could barely hold on to her charcoal pencil. Seeing Yaro naked was nothing like seeing Kyle naked.

Courtney, meanwhile, was having no issue whatsoever.

The teacher walked around and observed Courtney drawing. "Very nice," she said. "Where do you go to art school?"

"I don't," Courtney said.

"You should. You have a natural gift. Don't waste it."

Courtney beamed with pride.

Yaro, who was naked on the platform mere feet away, said, "I want to see it. Show me, Courtney."

"Shh," his mother said. "No talking to the model, and no talking *from* the model. Next pose." She waved for Yaro to move.

Yaro shifted into another pose. Or so Perry had to guess, based on the changes in the shadows beneath his feet. She didn't dare look at his nude form. There was a small object on the floor that was either a raisin or a pebble, and she would get to the bottom of the mystery by the end of the life drawing session, even if it meant never taking her eyes off the floor.

Gabrielle Banks leaned in front of Perry and gently lifted the young woman's chin up with her finger. "You have to look, dear. You have to see before you can draw."

Perry was suddenly confronted with a naked Yaro Banks. And all of his business. The man had a lot of business going on. There was the business of his shapely buttocks, his muscular thighs, his narrow waist, and all the other stuff.

The young man's mother leaned in and whispered to Perry, "Just start where you can. Why don't you start small?"

"Small?" Perry's voice cracked. "I don't see anything small."

There were a few chuckles around the room. Yaro let out a big guffaw.

Courtney said, "Oh, Perry," and kept sketching her next masterpiece.

Gabrielle Banks said, "By small, I mean a small detail. Try sketching the line of the forearm or the calf, on its own."

"I can do that?"

"Of course you can. You don't have to draw everything," she said. "It's like life. Start somewhere. The important thing is to begin."

Perry wiped the sweat off her fingertips, adjusted her grip on the charcoal, and started. The teacher's quiet reassurance emboldened her to try drawing Yaro's calf muscle, with its horseshoe-shaped indentation. She'd gotten to the knee when the teacher called out for the next pose change.

"Don't worry about capturing detail," she said, walking around the circle. "Try to capture the overall gesture, the sense of motion."

Yaro settled into his next pose. Perry picked a detail. His forearm and fist.

Perry made bold, heavy strokes on her canvas.

After half a minute, Courtney leaned over, looked at Perry's work, and said, "You lusty badger!"

"What?"

"Wow. I wasn't going to go there, but you really went there. That's quite the imagination you have."

Perry tilted her head to the side and looked at the shapes on her paper. She'd been drawing Yaro's forearm, and not very well. But, thanks to her bold, simple strokes, it appeared that she had drawn the most businesslike aspect of the young man's business.

Perry stifled a scream of horror and flipped her sheet over to a fresh one.

Yaro said, "That one, I definitely want to see."

"Shh," his mother said, and she slapped her son on the bottom.

"No touching," he snapped at her.

"No talking," she snapped back.

When the pose ended, Gabrielle Banks said, "Next, our *very quiet* model will take poses that are less dynamic so he can maintain them for longer periods. We'll start with a classic seated pose." She passed him a stool and a piece of paper towel to put on top as a barrier. Yaro took a seat and took a more relaxed pose, one that would be easy to keep for twenty minutes while everyone sketched.

Perry's initial shock over Yaro's nudity passed, and the whole situation started to feel normal. She was just a student, sitting in a classroom, learning how to do something.

Someone got up to turn off a leaking tap in the kitchenette counter along one side of the classroom. It was such a normal classroom activity that it further relaxed her.

Perry managed to survey her surroundings and think about something other than Yaro's naked body. How many purposes did the room serve? One wall held a collection of ukeleles and tambourines. Another wall held decorated masks with eyeholes.

Yaro finished his second long pose, and the class took a break.

"The door will be unlocked for fifteen minutes," Gabrielle Banks said. "Use your time wisely."

Yaro pulled on a loosely tied robe for the duration of the break, which made him seem even more naked to Perry. She knew he was naked under the thin layer of terry cloth, and somehow that was more distracting.

The old man, Larry, approached the girls and said, "Would either of you two young ladies like to smoke some medical marijuana with me? My treat."

Courtney said, "No, but I'll come stand outside with you to cool down. This room is warm." She stood and looked at Perry expectantly.

"I'll stay," Perry said. "I have to show Yaro the picture I drew of his arm."

Courtney raised her eyebrows but didn't say anything. She left with Larry.

Perry flipped through her drawings. She showed Yaro the drawing that had made Courtney accuse Perry of being a lusty badger.

Yaro choked and spat out some of the grape soda he'd been drinking. "That's not an arm," he said. "Not my arm, anyway. Where are the fingers?"

"Don't make fun of me. I'm not very good at drawing, but at least I was trying."

"Trying with your eyes closed?"

"I was looking right at your arm when I drew it. You must have moved it on me."

His dark eyes sparkled. "I hold very still on my seated poses. Judging by the look of this masterpiece, you must have been thinking about something else."

"No," she said.

"That's not an arm."

"Of course it is. I'll add the fingers," she said, reaching for the charcoal.

"Don't you dare." He ripped the sheet off the pad of paper. "I'm keeping this. Will you sign it for me?"

She rolled her eyes and protested, but she did sign it for him.

He asked, "What else have you got? Show me."

She flipped to the drawing of his calf. "There's this. Can you tell what it is?"

"Yes. It's so obvious. That's my butt."

"No. It's your calf."

"Why is there a crack down the middle?"

"That's not a crack. It's this line." She leaned forward and poked him on the back of his calf. His skin was surprisingly hot.

"No touching," he said softly. "No touching the model."

She jerked her hand back. "I didn't mean it."

He gazed into her eyes. "I didn't mind."

Perry started having the funny feelings again.

He was so close to her, and so naked underneath the robe.

She pushed her chair back and stood. "Where did you get that grape soda?"

"There's a vending machine in the hallway." He leaned forward to get up. "I'll go with you."

"No need," she said, and raced out of the room.

Perry stayed in the hallway and drank her grape soda until it was time for the class to start again.

Once everyone was back in their seats, Gabrielle Banks locked the door and turned off half of the lights.

"Let's try some more dramatic shadows for our final sketches," she said. "Are there any requests for any specific poses?"

A woman with red dreadlocks raised her hand and asked for a specific pose. "I'm working on backs," the woman explained.

Larry grumbled, "But I'm working on fronts."

"Then move your chair around, Larry," the teacher said. "We work in a circle for a reason."

Perry raised her hand. "We can do that? We can move our chairs?"

"Of course. Just get it out of the way before we begin sketching so you don't distract the others."

Yaro made eye contact with Perry and raised an eyebrow. He watched her as she picked up her chair and circled around to where he couldn't make eye contact.

The group began sketching.

The teacher came by and said to Perry, "So, you're the young lady with the textile art. It's wonderful work. I can't wait to see more." She studied the awkward charcoal lines on Perry's paper. "Keep working at this. You may not be a natural at drawing, but there's something special inside you."

"When do I pay you the twelve dollars?"

"Your first one is free," the teacher said warmly. "That's how a good dealer gets her customers hooked." She glanced over at her son then back at Perry. Softly, so Yaro couldn't hear, she said, "My son always befriends the most lovely young women. You look exactly like that singer, Jade."

"I get that a lot."

"You should let my son draw you sometime. He does wonderful figurative work. Perhaps the three of us could meet up on a weekday evening, and I could draw you as well. You have wonderful cheekbones."

"Thank you."

"Keep drawing," she said, waving to Perry's motionless hand. "Everything gets better with practice."

Chapter 18

Sunday

The next day at work, Donny and Toph listened very closely as Perry told them about her and Courtney's nude drawing class with Yaro Banks.

Perry hoped that Donny, the older and happily married cook, would have some good perspective on Yaro's motivations. She didn't expect much from young Toph.

She said to the guys, "Based on that, would you guys say he likes me as more than a friend?"

Donny rubbed his sideburns. "He was naked for how long in front of you?"

"Almost two hours."

"That's a long time to be naked." Donny shuddered. "Especially in a brightly lit room full of people."

"He didn't seem embarrassed at all."

Toph said, "If he was naked for two hours, you would know if he liked you, Perry. Trust me." Toph waggled his eyebrows. "You would know."

Donny laughed and clapped Toph on the back. "Kid, just because you have zero control over yourself doesn't mean that every guy is the same way."

Toph snorted. "I have some control."

Perry and Donny stared at him.

"Okay. I have no control, but I'm working on it," Toph said. "I will have myself under control someday. It would be a lot easier if I had a girlfriend who could help me tame my dragon."

Perry said, "Please don't call it a dragon, Toph. No talk about taming it, either. Please don't ruin another enjoyable movie franchise for me."

"Toph, don't talk about it at all," Donny said. "I haven't had breakfast yet."

"You two are uptight," Toph said. "The human body is natural and beautiful."

"Not when it's yours," Donny said.

"At least I'm not old like you," Toph said. "At least I still have control over my butt. At least I can go a full hour without farting."

Donny frowned at Toph. "Dude. What happens in the kitchen stays in the kitchen."

"Not if it wafts over to the dishwashing station," Toph said.

"That's enough," Perry said. "I deeply regret coming to you two for relationship advice."

"Don't say that," Donny said. He put his arm around the skinny prep cook. "Toph and I have a beautiful relationship." He gazed deeply into Toph's eyes. "Don't we, lover?"

"Hold me like you mean it," Toph said.

"I'll hold you like I mean it," Donny growled, squeezing the kid tighter. "And I'll kiss you like I mean it, too."

Toph sighed. "I love the way your sideburns smell like rancid vegetable oil."

"I love the way you fetch my pickles when I yell at you."

"I love the way you yell at me to fetch your pickles."

"I've got one special dill pickle for you, Toph."

Perry said, "I'm leaving before this gets any weirder."

As she left the kitchen, the guys were making kissing sounds. Or kissing. She didn't look back.

Perry found Courtney in the dining room, cleaning menus and trying to avoid eye contact with the hungry customers who were already lined up outside.

The weekend line for brunch at Delilah's could extend all the way down the block on sunny days. During the winter months, it was possible for the diner to be open for a few minutes on Sunday morning before the first party showed up. The weather had warmed up recently, though, and the customers were there.

Perry eyed the crowd on the other side of the glass doors and asked Courtney, "Do you ever get the eerie feeling you're in one of those zombie movies?"

"Don't make eye contact," Courtney said. "We've got five more minutes. Don't you dare cave in and open the door early."

"Opening time is only five minutes from now. What's the difference? We're both here anyway."

"Today, it's five minutes. Next week, it'll be ten minutes."

"We could open earlier, you know. I bet if we opened a full hour earlier, we'd still be more than busy enough for the first hour to cover the extra wages."

"But then people wouldn't line up," Courtney said. "Don't you know the first principle of customer manipulation? People always want what they can't have. Delilah's isn't popular in spite of the lineups. It's popular *because* of them."

"I never realized how cynical you were," Perry said.

Courtney's tone was as short and snappy as the short side of her asymmetrical haircut. "I'm not cynical. I'm realistic."

"What's the attitude all about? Are you mad at me?"

"Maybe." Courtney aggressively cleaned the menus for the second time.

"What did I do this time?"

Courtney slumped her shoulders and set down the cleaning spray. "Nothing," she said. "Nothing but regularly make more tips than me lately. Plus you have all the cute guys falling in love with you instead of me. Couldn't you at least leave me one?"

"You can have Yaro. I don't want him."

"That's what you say now, but you'll change your mind."

"We can start pooling our tips again, like we used to. I don't even care about the tips. You can have some of mine. We always help with each other's tables anyway."

"I can't let you do that."

One of the customers waiting in line tapped on the glass and pointed to his watch.

Both girls pointed to the clock on the back wall. The clock was wrong, but it was the only time that mattered inside Delilah's Universe.

Perry said, "I thought things were heating up with you and Yaro. He was definitely flirting with you after the drawing class."

Courtney scrubbed a table she'd already cleaned.

Perry asked, "Did something happen after he dropped me off at my house and drove you home? Did he say something horrible about your drawings?"

"No," Courtney said, pouting. "He said I had a real talent for drawing."

"You do."

"He drove me home and was a perfect gentleman. Then I invited him inside for some homemade cookies."

"Now I know you're lying. Your parents don't keep cookies in the house, let alone homemade ones."

"We have some low-carb ones made with almond flour."

"What happened? Did he go inside?"

"He did," Courtney said. "He liked the cookies."

"Why are you upset? Did he eat all of them?"

"My parents were out, so I showed him my room."

"Uh-oh," Perry said. Once Courtney showed a guy her room, things tended to escalate quickly. "Did he storm your castle?"

"He didn't get past the moat," Courtney said. "We just kissed and talked for about an hour."

"He likes you! I'm so glad. Now you can let go of your paranoia that he's trying to get my drawbridge down."

Courtney wrinkled her nose. "He didn't even *try* to get past my piranhas."

"I don't get it. Would you have been happier if you'd had to fight him off?"

"Of course not." She frowned. "Do you think that's it? Do you think there's something wrong with me?"

"Why are you asking me? I've had zero relationships."

"I'm asking you because I already asked Donny and Toph, and they weren't helpful at all."

"Did they pretend to make out with each other in front of you?"

She nodded. "We need to make some better career choices. We can't work here forever, Perry. It's like we're still in high school."

"This is way better than high school. We get paid, and there's no homework."

"We need to make better *life* choices," Courtney said.

"Now you sound like your parents."

"Kill me now," Courtney said.

They both turned and looked at the big clock. The minute hand ticked onto the hour.

The door began to rattle as the impatient customers tried to open it.

Perry said, "It's always funny when the zombies think the door's going to open on its own."

"It was funny the first hundred times I saw it happen," Courtney said. "Now it's starting to get old."

"I think *you're* starting to get old."

"Maybe." Courtney walked over to the door and twisted the deadbolt.

Chapter 19

Monday

Perry Langtree walked in to work early Monday morning. The kitchen was still dark. She found Donny, the cook, in the waitress station, crouched in front of the coffee maker, watching it brew.

"I'm glad you're keeping both eyes on that thing," she said. "It brews much faster when you stare at it." She hopped up on the counter and watched it, too. "Donny, why do you drink so much coffee?"

"Because I'm a grown man and I have grown man problems."

"Such as what? Do you have hair growing in your ears? My dad has that problem."

"Do you remember yesterday when I was pretending to kiss Toph?"

"Remember? I've been trying really hard to forget."

"Well, things went a little far."

"What are you talking about?"

"You know how we were teasing the kid about having no control over his dragon?"

Perry didn't say anything. Her mind was already filling in the rest of the story.

"I felt it on my leg," Donny said. "The kid really doesn't have any control over it."

"Maybe you shouldn't have been holding him so tight and talking about kissing him."

Donny raised an eyebrow. "You think?"

They watched the coffee brew for a few more minutes.

"Working in a busy kitchen is a high-stress environment," Donny said. "People joke around. It's what kitchens are like. Nobody would stick around for the long hours and the low pay alone. Having fun is essential." Donny looked at Perry. "If I've ever said or done anything that made you uncomfortable, I'm very sorry."

"I don't consider the sort of stuff you guys do harassment."

"But does it make you uncomfortable?"

"Sometimes."

Donny looked crestfallen.

"But I'm eighteen and I've never been kissed," Perry said. "Everything people do makes me uncomfortable."

"Really? But you act so self-assured and confident. You seem like one of those people who's never bothered by anything."

"It's all an act," Perry said.

"You're good at your act," he said. "Sometimes I forget who your grandma is, but sometimes, like now, you remind me."

"Back it up to yesterday. Were you and Toph just talking about kissing, or were you actually kissing?"

Donny looked away. "We may have kissed."

"You didn't."

"We did. But only because we thought you were still standing there." He crossed his arms. "This is all your fault."

Perry snorted. "Was there tongue involved?"

Donny made a retching sound. "Not *my* tongue. But the kid has no control over himself."

Perry patted Donny on the shoulder. "I'm sure your wife will forgive you for cheating on her. She needs to come down here and meet Toph in person to see that he doesn't pose a threat to your marriage."

"Oh, my wife thought it was *hilarious*. She's like you, Perry. Great sense of humor. She needs it, to put up with me."

The coffee finished brewing. Donny poured himself a cup, blew over it, and took a noisy sip. "I need to examine my life choices."

"That sentiment seems to be trending," Perry said.

She grabbed a cup of her own and filled it halfway. She didn't love or hate coffee. She only drank it because it was right there, and it was free for all the staff.

"Toph is worried," Donny said.

"Worried that you're going to press harassment charges? He should have thought about that before he stuck his tongue in your mouth."

"No. He's worried that he might not be into girls. He always thought he was, but after Sunday, and the way he reacted to me, he was feeling confused."

"We do live in confusing times," Perry said.

"He needs to kiss an actual girl," Donny said. Then he gave Perry a hopeful look.

"No way," Perry said.

"Why not? You've never kissed a guy, and he's never kissed a girl. I'm not suggesting you do anything regrettable that leads to human offspring, but you two should kiss."

"No."

Donny dug into his pocket and pulled out a handful of change. "I'll pay you," he said. "Please?"

"Offering me a handful of quarters and blue dryer lint is not making your proposal any better," she said. "Besides, I charge way more than that."

"How much?"

"I'm just kidding, Donny. I'm not going to kiss Toph just so the two of you can get over him dry humping your leg."

Donny gasped and took a step back. "How did you know he humped my leg? Were you still standing there? You were, weren't you?"

"I..." She had no words.

Donny's serious expression broke. He laughed and pointed at Perry. "Got you," he said. "Totally got you."

She sighed. "You fibber. Were you putting me on about the whole thing?"

"Just the last bit about the dry humping. The rest happened. Which is why I'm going to come up with a way to get you two crazy kids to kiss each other." Donny tapped his forehead. "I've got a lot more up here besides recipes for chipped beef."

"Please don't involve me in one of your wacky schemes."

"I have to do something. I have to help the kid. It's my fault for having such dreamy eyes and kissable lips."

"Don't try to trick me, though."

"I'll do what I have to do."

"Listen, Donny. I'll make you a deal, okay? If I haven't kissed anyone within a reasonable amount of time, I'll kiss Toph."

"Are you messing with me?"

"I'm stone-cold serious. We'll go into the walk-in cooler, turn off the lights, and make out for a full five minutes."

Donny rubbed his hands together. "Now we're talking!" He started pacing. "I'll set up some mood lighting inside the cooler. I can get some of those twinkle lights to string overhead."

"Don't get ahead of yourself. It's not happening anytime soon. I need a reasonable amount of time to find someone to kiss on my own." Perry straightened her posture. "This is good motivation for me. I should have done this a long time ago."

"How much time do you need?"

"How about until Christmas?"

"Too long," he said. "I'll give you until the summer solstice."

"Sure. Wait. When is that?"

"It shifts around a couple days. It's either before, on, or after June twenty-first."

"Sure," Perry said. "Let's call it the twenty-first. I can find someone to kiss before June twenty-first." She pointed at Donny. "Start saving up your loose change."

"I thought you weren't charging me."

"I'm not. But you may have to pay some other girl to smooch your confused lover for you."

"Oh," Donny said, nodding. "That's a good point. I can put the money from the swear jar toward an escort service instead of beer." He patted his belly. "This is just the motivation I needed to cut back on the liquid carbs."

Perry pointed to the sign that banned the discussion of carbs.

Donny rolled his eyes. "We're not even open yet."

He topped up his coffee then went back to the kitchen to prep for the morning service.

Courtney arrived a few minutes later.

"How's it going with Yaro?" Perry asked. "I hope he said something nice so you don't have to mope about it all day today."

"He sent me some flirty messages."

"That's good."

"Honestly, I don't know."

"I've never seen you get hung up on a guy like this."

"I know," she said. "Maybe this one's special. You think he might be The One?"

"We are way too young to be talking about meeting The One."

"My parents were already married by the time they were the age we are now."

"Do you think dating was easier twenty years ago?"

"I don't think it was ever easy," Courtney said.

The girls got the dining room ready, turned on the lights, and unlocked the door.

Because it was Monday, there was no brunch lineup.

The dining room remained empty a full ten minutes before the first customer of the day arrived.

"Here comes your boyfriend," Courtney said to Perry.

Perry didn't know which one Courtney meant until she looked up and saw Marcus walking in the door, newspaper in hand.

Chapter 20

"Good morning, Crossword Guy," Perry said. This was her second Monday seeing him since learning his real name, but she liked the nickname.

He pushed his thick-rimmed glasses up his nose and smiled. "Good morning, Funny Waitress."

"Your usual table, sir?"

"Unless they're fumigating it for rats."

"Fumigation is for insects. We use high-quality humane traps for the rats. It doesn't ruin the meat quality for the daily soup special."

Marcus wrinkled his nose and took his usual seat.

He asked, "What's new?"

"Not the deep fryer oil," she said. "But our special today is apple spice pancakes."

"Can I get that with a side of bacon and poached eggs?"

"You sure can, sweetie."

Marcus's jaw dropped. "You sounded just like Lana Langtree when you said that."

"Ain't you darlin' with all your compliments!"

He shook his head like a cartoon dog.

When Perry came back with more coffee, Marcus said, "Thanks again for letting me pick your dad's brain last week. I was meaning to stop in and see you before now, but I had a big paper that was not going well."

"School keeps you pretty busy, huh?"

"I skated through high school with straight A's no problem. University, however, is a whole new level. I barely have time to sleep and shower, let alone anything else." He gestured to the newspaper, which was open to the crossword puzzle. "Coming here on Mondays is my only break where I do nothing."

"Nothing but flirt with your waitress."

He cleared his throat and glanced out the window. "I never meant to do that," he said.

"Tell that to your flirty blue eyes and your nice smile."

He rubbed the back of his neck, still facing the window. "Perry, I'm pretty busy with school right now, plus you're eighteen and I'm twenty-one."

Perry remembered what Yaro had told her about the age difference. They hadn't talked about Marcus much at all on Saturday, but on the drive home Yaro had mentioned that the Philby family were in the public eye and that Lance Philby, the city's most popular weatherman, didn't want his son dating a teenager.

Perry slyly used that information to inform what she said next.

"I'll be nineteen soon," Perry said.

Marcus gave her a surprised look. "You will?"

"That's how time works," she said, and she walked away, smiling.

Some more customers came in, and Perry got too busy to chat much more with Marcus.

She did refill his coffee cup several times, and he took his time on the crossword puzzle. She enjoyed having him there, even if they weren't interacting. She didn't know it, but he felt the exact same way.

When Marcus did leave, he said, "See you next Monday."

"Only if I'm working that day."

He paused, frowning.

"Which I am," she said.

He looked relieved. He smiled then left.

When Perry got back to the privacy of the kitchen to grab some food, Courtney said, "You should have written your phone number on his bill. Or just given it to him."

"If I want to harass the young man using modern technology, I can get his number from his best friend," Perry said.

Toph asked, "Why don't you do that? I'd love it if some girl sent me messages." He grinned. "And pictures."

Perry gave Toph a raised eyebrow. "Are you sure about that? Girls, huh? What about grown men with sideburns?"

Toph's face reddened. He disappeared into the walk-in cooler.

Donny, who'd been listening in between flipping burgers, said, "I approve of your strategy, Perry. Don't give him your number until he asks. Play hard to get."

Perry pointed a french fry at the cook. "You're only saying that to manipulate me. You don't approve of games. You told me. You want me to totally blow it with Crossword Guy so that you don't have to pay an escort to make a man out of Toph."

Courtney raised her hand. "Excuse me? Did I miss something?"

Donny said, "He kissed me. Hard. With tongue."

Courtney said, "I changed my mind. I don't want to know."

Perry and Donny explained everything to Courtney despite her protests. They were in the lull before the lunch rush and needed something to do anyway.

Courtney summarized. "So, if Perry doesn't kiss a guy before June twenty-first, she has to kiss Toph in the cooler? Does he know about this?"

"Yes," Donny said. "It's the only thing keeping him from quitting. He can't quit. I need him."

Courtney waggled her eyebrows. "I bet you do."

"He's been upset ever since the kiss." Donny rubbed the sides of his mouth. "I should know better than to flex my powers of seduction on anyone who hasn't built up tolerance."

The waitresses exchanged a look then got back to gobbling down their pre-lunch-rush food.

Chapter 21

Tuesday

Perry Langtree was wiping children's face prints off the glass at the front of the diner when the first customer of the day walked in.

It was Sunshine Banks, Yaro's sister. Sunshine also resembled their mother, with dark skin, a long face, and a wide nose. She had very full lips and was stunning. Her hair was black at the roots and faded blue on the tips.

"There you are," Sunshine said. "Yaro told me I could find you here."

"He told you? Now where am I supposed to hide out from my legions of fans and paparazzi?"

"Your secret is safe with me." She extended her hand. "I'm Sunshine Banks."

"Perry Langtree."

"You sure are," Sunshine said, looking her over. "I can't figure out if you look more like your grandma or your mom. You're so lucky to come from such a great pedigree."

"Hey. Don't say that. I met your mom, and she's a pretty cool lady."

Sunshine flashed her eyes. "Yeah. I heard all about that. My mother won't stop going on about the talented textile artist and her naturally gifted friend." Sunshine glanced around. "Is the other one here? I don't think I saw her with you at Yaro's art show."

"She didn't come with me that night. Courtney will be in later. I'll tell her you said hi. We both had a lot of fun hanging out with your brother on Saturday."

"I heard," Sunshine said.

"Is he coming in today?" Perry glanced at the door.

"Just me," Sunshine said. "Do you have any low-carb options?"

"I recommend the place across the street."

Sunshine shrugged. "I'm here already. Do I just sit anywhere?"

"Anywhere but the big booths."

Sunshine headed for the bar by the waitress station and sat where Yaro had sat the week before.

She leaned over, peered through the pass-through window into the kitchen, and waved at Donny.

"Hey, Mr. Chef," she said. "I like your sideburns. What's fresh today?"

Donny leaned out, grinning. He loved it when customers noticed him back there, especially if they were pretty girls.

"The tomatoes are perfect," he said. "How would you like me to make you a nice vegetable omelet with a side of fresh guacamole?"

"Sold," Sunshine said, then she blew him a kiss. Next, she leaned forward, draping her body over the counter, and rummaged around the collection of staff mugs, selecting the red one. "Fill 'er up," she said to Perry, holding the mug out for coffee.

"Those are the staff mugs," Perry said.

"So? I like this red one. I don't like diner cups. They look like teacups. Charge me extra if you want."

Perry filled the mug, but something about the interaction didn't sit right with her. At Delilah's, the staff wanted customers to be comfortable, but not too comfortable.

Perry turned away briefly to punch in the omelet. There was no vegetable omelet with guacamole on the menu, so she punched it in as the daily special.

Donny was having difficulty frying the vegetables and gawking through the window at Sunshine at the same time. It got even more difficult when Toph came over to also stare at Sunshine.

Donny growled at Toph to stop grinding against him, and the two began arguing in hushed tones while competing for the window.

Sunshine smiled and watched the guys as she sipped her coffee from the red staff mug.

"Fun place," she said.

Perry replied, "Every day around here is an adventure."

"This restaurant must do really well. There's always a big lineup on the weekend." Sunshine glanced over the empty dining room. "Is it always this dead on weekday mornings?"

"Tuesdays are slow. The owners have some ideas for promotions."

"Don't change a thing. This place is perfect how it is," Sunshine said. "It's the ultimate mix of high and low end. You should never mess with perfection."

"Do you work in the neighborhood?"

"I work all over. I do deliveries for my uncle's art gallery."

"Your whole family is in the art business?"

"Yup." She set down her mug and pursed her full lips into a pucker that bordered on a pout. Flatly, she said, "Lucky me."

"Are you not interested in art?"

"Not that kind of art. I'm actually a singer."

"Oh." Perry froze and said nothing more. Growing up as the daughter of a famous singer and the granddaughter of an even more famous singer, she had learned that the phrase "I'm a singer" was usually followed by a plea for advice, or for some sort of favor from Perry's famous relatives.

"This coffee isn't bad," Sunshine said.

Perry started breathing again, relieved that one of those uncomfortable requests wasn't forthcoming.

"Glad you like it," Perry said. "I made a fresh pot instead of microwaving yesterday's leftovers."

Sunshine laughed.

Perry liked her laugh. It was like Yaro's and their mother's. It put Perry at ease.

Sunshine said, "I hear you like Marcus Philby."

Perry felt less at ease. "He's one of our regulars. He comes in on Mondays with his crossword puzzle."

"That sounds like Marcus, all right. Does he order the exact same thing every time?"

"Usually, but yesterday he took a chance on the apple spice pancakes. I was so proud of him."

Sunshine grinned. "Were you, now?"

Perry got the sense she was being mocked. She looked away from Sunshine and rearranged the staff mugs, shoving them deeper under the counter where it would be harder for customers to reach them.

"Marcus is slow to warm up to new things," Sunshine said. "But if you're patient, he might come around eventually."

"We're just friends," Perry said.

Toph emerged from the kitchen, carrying an enormous omelet and three sides' worth of guacamole.

"Ma'am," he said, hip-checking Perry out of the way so he could place the plate in front of Sunshine. "The chef has prepared this for you. There are three kinds of heirloom tomatoes, and goat cheese."

"Wow," Sunshine said. "This is too much for me to eat by myself. Do you want a bite?" She had cut off a piece and was holding it out to Toph on her fork.

Toph leaned forward, ate the bite, then ran back to the kitchen at top speed.

"That one's adorable," Sunshine said. "Kinda nervous, don't you think? Must be shy."

"That's not the first adjective that comes to mind when I think about Toph," Perry said.

Sunshine dug into her omelet and took a bite without even trying to wipe Toph's germs off the fork. "Mmm. That's good." She waved at Donny through the window and blew him another kiss. "Wonderful!"

The door chimed, and the next customers arrived.

Perry got busy and didn't get to chat much more with Sunshine. Yaro's sister finished her omelet and then walked into the kitchen to chat with the guys just long enough for the first of the mid-morning rush orders to pile up.

Sunshine finally left the kitchen, paid her bill using her uncle's art gallery credit card, then hugged Perry.

She hugged Perry for a long time, considering they didn't know each other.

"You're so huggable," Sunshine said into Perry's ear. "Be patient with Marcus. He'll come around." Then she pulled away, looked Perry over, and said, "I love this waitress look on you."

Before Perry could say anything else, Sunshine was back out the front door again, off to deliver art.

The next time Perry passed within earshot of the kitchen, she was hit with a dozen questions about her new friend.

Chapter 22

Things at the Langtree house were starting to feel normal.

It was Perry's third week of filling in for her mother, and Perry was keeping up with the instruction binder. She was halfway through her five-week assignment. Apart from a few laundry blunders, she was doing a great job. Most girls her age would have been serving frozen dinners and letting the housework slide, but Perry had kept up her end of the bargain with her mother.

As all three current residents of the Langtree house were digging into the soup, made with a minimal number of carrot slices to keep the guys from complaining, all three of their phones buzzed or beeped with incoming messages.

"That'll be your mother," Dale Langtree said.

"Mommy," Perry said.

"Mommy!" Garnet cried excitedly. All three raced to get their phones out.

The text was, indeed, from Mrs. Langtree, known to the world simply as Jade.

It read: *Bad news, family. I need to stay here in LA for at least another month. I'm really sorry and I miss you all so much it hurts. Hugs and Kisses!*

As Perry read the message, a wave of disgust passed over her body, settling in her stomach. She pushed her bowl of soup away. Who needed soup? Or food? She might never feel hungry again.

Garnet started to cry. Not little baby tears down his cheeks, either. He flat-out bawled, his mouth turning down in a grimace. He was racked with sobs.

Perry went to her brother, held him, and let him blubber on her. "Poor monkey," she said over and over.

Their father, Dale Langtree, set his phone on the table and resumed eating his soup.

"This is better than how your mother makes it," he said of the soup, which only set off Garnet's wails again.

Perry said, "Dad! That's all you've got to say?"

"I just live here." He kept eating. Then he picked up his empty bowl and spoon and put them away into the dishwasher.

Garnet wiped his nose and face with Perry's shirt. "Dad! You can't let her do this to us."

"Your mother's a free spirit," Dale said, his voice eerily calm. "She can't soar with the eagles if she's stuck down here with us turkeys."

Garnet sobbed pitifully.

"You know what? We don't have to stay here at the house," Perry said to her brother, trying to sound upbeat for his benefit. "We can fly down there for a visit. I've got some money saved up. What do you think of that?"

"Really?" Garnet's nose blew a bubble.

Dale said, "She doesn't want her children there."

Perry glared at her father. "Don't make this worse than it has to be."

"Peridot, you and I both know that when your mother said she'd be gone for five weeks, she was lying."

"Maybe she was being optimistic, but she wasn't lying."

"I've known her a lot longer than you have. Let me ask you something. Did I look at all surprised when we got that message?"

"I was looking at my phone, Dad. Then I was looking at Garnet. I wasn't studying your microexpressions."

Garnet started wailing again. Perry dabbed his face with a napkin, not that it did much good. Garnet was a messy cryer.

Dale said, "Thank you for taking care of your brother. Don't worry about me. I can take care of myself." He took a few steps toward his computer den then turned and went in the direction of the front door. Perry heard his keys jingle then the front door open and close.

Garnet pulled away from Perry and ran to the cupboard where they kept the chocolate and other junk food.

"Get out of there until after you've finished your soup," Perry said.

Garnet ignored her and started eating cookies.

Perry dumped his bowl of soup back into the pot. "Fine. You can eat this tomorrow."

Garnet increased the speed of his cookie consumption.

Perry said, "We can talk about everything when Dad gets back from his drive."

"Talking doesn't do anything," Garnet said, spraying cookie crumbs everywhere.

"Now you sound exactly like Dad."

"Yeah? Well, you sound exactly like Mom, and I'm not very happy with her right now."

"No kidding. Me neither."

He narrowed his eyes. "I don't need you. I can take care of myself."

"Why are you giving me the attitude? I'm not Mom. I'm the person who's still here, trying to hold this house together. Don't be mad at me."

"You made her go away," he said. "You told her it was a good idea for her to do the show."

"Have you *met* our mother? Jade does what she wants."

"You're dead to me," he said, moving on from the cupboard to the freezer.

Perry said, "You'd better find a nicer way to express your feelings than being snarky at me, young man. If you keep this up, I'm going to yank off both of your pudgy little arms and beat you to death with them."

He grabbed a carton of ice cream from the freezer and a big spoon from the drawer.

"At least use a bowl," Perry said.

Garnet didn't use a bowl. He took the ice cream and the spoon and left for his room.

She yelled after him, "Don't stop until you eat the whole thing and throw up!"

He yelled back that he would.

Alone in the kitchen, Perry tried to eat the soup but couldn't. Her head was buzzing. The soup was like brown water. Either she'd made the worst soup in Langtree family history or her taste buds weren't working.

She picked up her phone and read the message from Jade again.

It hadn't gotten any better.

As Perry was plotting her reply, a message came in from Yaro Banks.

It was a photo of a painting he was working on. The canvas was entirely shades of blue.

He sent a text as well: *Do you think it needs more blue?*

She wrote back: *You can never have too much blue.*

Yaro: *My sister keeps raving about how cool you are.*

Perry: *I am pretty cool, unlike my mother, who is actually the worst.*

Yaro: *Did something happen?*

Perry: *It's complicated.*

Yaro: *Are you home now? I'll come pick you up. You need to see this canvas in person.*

Perry agreed.

Yaro pulled up in front of the house twenty minutes later. He was driving the yellow Range Rover again.

Just seeing the bright-colored vehicle cheered up Perry.

And then seeing Yaro's smiling face made her feel like maybe everything else was going to be okay.

Chapter 23

"It's the exact right amount of blue," Perry said.

She and Yaro Banks were sitting on a paint-spattered leather couch inside his rented art studio. The studio was in a noisy part of town, inside a converted former paint factory. Yaro had his own space within a cooperative with several other artists, including his mother. Gabrielle Banks wasn't in the studio that evening, but lots of other people were milling around, taking trips to the shared sink to wash paintbrushes and make more coffee.

Perry was happy to be there. All her feelings about her mother's text message about staying in LA at least another month were miles away, back at the house.

"I'm glad you like it," Yaro said of the painting.

"Who said I liked it?" She gave him a teasing look.

He tossed a paint-spattered cloth at her playfully.

"It's beautiful," she said in a serious tone. "Is it possible that after taking one drawing class from your mother, and finding out how hard it is to draw anything, I'm more able to appreciate art now?"

"Yes."

She turned her head and studied the canvas again. Why had she even been upset about a text message from her mom? It was only words on a screen. The future was going to be whatever it would be. Like how the blue painting was blue. It simply was.

Yaro said, "You have a great profile. Who does your brother look like?"

"Funny you should ask. My brother, Garnet, doesn't look like anyone in the family. He's got black hair, and his face shape isn't like my mom's, or my dad's. That's why we had the whole Paternity Incident."

"The what?"

"It's kind of embarrassing."

"Now you have to tell me. I need to know."

"My dad sent some samples to one of those mail-order DNA places."

"Uh-oh." Yaro grimaced. "Yikes."

"Oh, it was good news. The test came back showing that my father is Garnet's biological parent. The bad news is my dad used the credit card to pay for the test. My mom saw the charge on the statement and figured out the rest."

"Was she mad?"

"Not much at first. But my dad made it so much worse by lying and saying the DNA test was for someone at work. There was a lot of yelling that summer."

"That must be weird. I never heard my parents fight."

"Lucky you. My dad slept in one of the spare rooms long enough that my brother and I figured that was just how things were going to be forever. Then, one day, we came home from school and found the two of them giggling in the bath tub together. Like nothing had ever happened. Things have been okay since then." She looked down at her hands and picked at a hangnail. "Well, until now. He told me things haven't been great, and now I don't know when she's coming back, or even if she's coming back."

"She'll come back. She's your mom."

"But she's also Jade. Have you not heard her songs? Half of them are about being an independent woman, and the other half sound like alley cats in heat."

Yaro smirked. "I like the video of her setting her mean ol' ex-husband's suitcase on fire."

"My dad hates that one." Perry put her face in her hands and rubbed her temples. "Ugh. I came out with you to forget about it, and now I'm talking about it." She smacked her face. "What is wrong with me?"

"I know what will cheer you up," Yaro said.

"I'm not sure I want to be cheered up."

Yaro jumped up and grabbed something from behind a large canvas. It was a framed print.

He said, "Don't look at this unless you want to be cheered up."

Perry looked. It was the picture she had drawn of his arm. The arm that didn't look like an arm.

She jumped up. "You need to rip that up, not frame it!" She tried to get it from him, but Yaro had a much longer reach than Perry.

"It's priceless," he said. "I'm going to treasure it forever, right up until I sell it at auction for big bucks."

"You are twisted," she howled.

They fought like small children over the painting, Yaro holding it out of reach while Perry tried to get it by any means necessary.

Some of the other artists from the cooperative came in to see what the fuss was all about. Yaro showed the print and explained how it had come about.

The other artists were delighted by the drawing, as well as the fact Yaro had gotten it professionally framed.

A boy in skinny jeans told Perry she had a great future in the art world.

"I'm more of a textile artist than an illustrator," she said.

Skinny Jeans said, "We've got a room open for a textile artist. You should apply! It beats working at home. There's so much more energy down here, and we all collaborate."

Yaro said, "You should apply, Perry. I've shown some people your monsters, and everyone loves them."

Skinny Jeans looked at her with wide eyes. "You're the girl who does the monsters? I love them. You have to get a space here."

A tall woman with white hair said, "You've got my support. We could use some more female energy around here."

Yaro caught Perry's eye through the gathering crowd and smiled.

She smiled back.

She was no longer thinking about the music video of her mother setting a man's suitcase on fire.

Chapter 24

Yaro dropped Perry off at home. She stood on the porch and waved as the bright-yellow Range Rover disappeared.

Inside, she found her brother and father asleep in the den with the television blaring.

She turned off the sound, which, ironically, caused her father to wake up immediately.

"I wasn't sleeping," he said defensively. "I was watching that."

She tossed him the remote control. "It works better when your eyes are open."

She grabbed her brother by the arms and hauled him into an upright position.

Garnet moaned, "I don't feel so good."

Perry wasn't surprised, given that he'd skipped his dinner and eaten cookies and ice cream and who knew what else.

"I might be sick," he said.

"You can sleep with the barf bucket next to your bed," she said.

"Can I sleep in your bed?"

"Sure. But if you barf on me, it will be the last thing you ever do."

Garnet agreed to the terms.

Perry dragged her kid brother upstairs then tucked him into her bed. She had no intention of returning to her room that evening, let alone her bed. It was a queen-sized mattress, but she'd rather sleep on the hard bed in the spare room than get kicked by her brother all night long, let alone thrown up on.

After making sure Garnet had the family's flu bucket handy, Perry went back downstairs and into the den.

Dale Langtree was watching the television and fighting sleep.

Perry said to her father, "If you want Mom to come home, you have to talk to her."

Tersely, he said, "I'm not having this conversation with you."

"This is exactly like the paternity thing. You think something's going on with Mom, but you won't talk to her about it, and everything's just going to blow up in your face."

Dale Langtree turned off the television, got up, and went to the kitchen.

Perry followed him into the kitchen and put on the kettle for tea.

He pointed at the kettle and asked, "What are you doing?"

"I'm making tea. Mom always makes tea for you when you're upset."

"I'm not upset, but I will have some tea if you're making it."

Perry pulled out the teapot and some boxes of non-caffeinated tea.

"Mom has to come back eventually," Perry said. "All her stuff is here. We've got her Grammy awards."

Perry's father didn't say anything.

"The first two weeks flew by," Perry said. "The next month will go by even faster."

"That's the problem. Time flies. You kids keep getting more and more grown up." He disappeared into his office, which was off the kitchen, and returned with his Best Dad in the Universe mug, which he cleaned with the scrub brush.

"Garnet is going through a growth spurt," Perry said. "She'd better not be gone too long. I may have to take the kid shopping for longer pants."

"Do you miss her?"

Perry didn't answer right away.

Dale said, "I don't miss her temperamental moods. Your cooking is just as good as hers. Maybe we're better off this way, just the three of us."

The kettle reached its boiling point. Perry poured the water into the teapot.

Dale said, "Maybe this is how it happens."

"How what happens?"

"Divorce," he said.

Perry stared at the water in the teapot as the brown stain from the rooibos spread out.

She asked her father, "Did you take your pills today?"

He snapped back, "Did you take yours?"

"All I take is vitamins."

"Because that's all most people need. You know what? I'm not sure those meds I take are doing me any favors."

"Listen, Dad. You're the adult, and I'm the kid. If you don't like what you're taking, talk to your doctor. If you're going off, I think you need to taper."

"Is that what you think, Dr. Peridot Langtree?"

"All I know is that when you randomly skip a day, things get a little dicey."

He fidgeted with the dishes out on the counter, rearranging them into a grid.

"Maybe I will taper off," he said.

"Do you need me to call and set up a doctor appointment?"

He looked up, surprised. "You'd do that?"

"The phone number is in the binder that Mom left."

He glowered at her. "Of course it is. Your mother thought of everything."

Perry picked up the binder and flipped through it until she reached the medical section. She showed it to her father.

"Don't call," he said. "I'll call them myself in the morning."

"I'll leave the binder open on the counter."

He poured some tea into his mug and left for his office.

"Good talk," Perry said to the empty kitchen.

Then she picked up her phone and sent Yaro a full report.

Chapter 25

Perry Langtree was yawning as she walked into work on Wednesday morning.

While her brother had been sleeping off his ice-cream-and-cookie hangover in her bed, she'd taken to the spare room, only to have her brother find her there and climb in. All night long, she had kept getting woken up by the sounds of his stomach gurgling—but never woken up enough to actually get out of the bed and find a new location.

Garnet was back to his usual self in the morning, but he did ask for extra nuts and vegetables in his school lunch instead of cookies.

Perry had eaten her brother's cookies for breakfast and wasn't feeling that smart about it when she walked into the kitchen at Delilah's and caught a whiff of yesterday's leftovers in the compost bin by the door.

Donny greeted her cheerfully. "Perry! You're here just in time to help me with something." He shook a white bucket then pulled back the lid slowly. "Can you smell this pepper and make sure it hasn't gone bad?"

She wasn't even near the bucket, and her eyes were watering.

"Nice try," Perry said. "I'm supposed to stick my face in there and smell the black pepper dust you just shook up? Who would be stupid enough to try that?"

Just then, Toph emerged from the staff washroom with red, puffy eyes. "Donny, I don't think you're supposed to inhale pepper clouds," Toph said, blowing his nose.

"Of course you are," Donny said, grinning proudly at Perry. "It's the only way to be sure it's fresh. Plus it'll put some hair on your chest."

"I already have hair on my chest," Toph said. "I have over fifteen hairs."

"Yeah?" Donny started grabbing at Toph's chest, trying to pinch the hairs.

"Go easy on the kid," Perry said. "Stop groping him. Isn't it enough you made him question his sexuality?"

Toph's eyes went round. "You told Perry everything? You told her about the you-know-what?"

Donny ruffled the kid's hair roughly. "Why do you think she agreed to kiss you in the walk-in cooler on the summer solstice?"

Toph's eyes got even wider. "That's really happening? I thought you were only saying it to make me feel better."

Perry put her hands on her hips. "Oh, it's happening, Toph. My lips on your face. You'd better take good care of your pretty mouth. You'd better not let it get chapped."

Toph stood there gaping, eyes watering from the pepper.

Donny said, "Of course it won't happen if Perry finds someone else to kiss her before then. But don't you worry, little buddy. I've got a backup plan. You remember my cousin, Rhonda? She filled in a few shifts for Maggie over the winter."

Toph frowned. "Isn't your cousin Rhonda ancient?"

"She's not ancient," Donny said. "It's the smoking habit that makes her sound that way."

"No offense, but I'd rather kiss Perry," Toph said.

Perry said, "I'd be offended if you didn't."

"Rhonda's a fine woman," Donny said. "Don't insult my family."

Toph shrugged. "I guess Rhonda would do. She wouldn't be smoking while we kissed, would she?" He grimaced and stuck out his tongue. "I wouldn't want her to blow smoke rings into my mouth." He blew his nose, wiped his watering eyes, then tilted his head to one side. "Then again, maybe I would like that. How would I know?"

Donny shook the pepper bucket again. "Toph, I think a rat might have gotten in here," he said. "Can you lean in and take a look?"

"Sure," Toph said, leaning over eagerly.

Perry left the kitchen quickly. There was only so much casual kitchen cruelty she could take.

She found Courtney in the empty dining room, looking at something on her phone.

"Hey," Perry said.

Courtney startled and dropped her phone on her lap.

"Guilty conscience," Perry said. "What were you looking at over there?" She picked up the sprayer and spritzed the new face prints that had appeared on the windows since the day before.

"Nothing," Courtney said guiltily.

"Liar."

"Nothing you'd want to know about."

Perry's skin prickled all over. Courtney didn't lie about much, which meant it could only be one thing.

Perry asked, "Is it about someone in my family?"

"Forget I was doing anything," Courtney said. "I know you don't like hearing about the gossip blogs. Most of what they post is trash, anyway."

"It's *always* trash, but you should tell me anyway," Perry said. "Grandma or Mom?"

"Not your grandma."

Perry's breath caught in her throat. "What has Jade done now?"

"Nothing. Probably. Your mom's always getting photographed with guys. It doesn't mean anything."

"If you're not going to tell me, you'll have to show me," Perry said.

"It might not even be her," Courtney said.

"Show me now." Perry left the window cleaner and held out her hand. "Come on. Let's get this over with and carry on with our day."

Courtney handed over her phone.

The headline screamed about *Jade's New Young Squeeze*.

And there she was, in living color. Jade. Perry's mother.

Perry skipped the text and went to the pictures. There were shots of Jade at a restaurant, sitting at a cozy table for two with an attractive guy—a musician, presumably—with dark hair and a chiseled profile. The guy reminded Perry of the famous action hero star, Jocko Ranger, but younger. Perry's mother and the guy looked friendly, but so what? It was Los Angeles. It was show business.

Perry scrolled down.

There were more shots of Jade and the same guy, getting progressively more intimate. They were wearing the same outfits as the dinner pictures. In the final photos, the two were seen kissing. The last picture was the man standing in front of Jade, apparently yelling at the cameraman. Behind him, Jade was holding her face in her hands.

Courtney said, "I know it looks bad, but they're just kissing. People make mistakes, and they kiss people they shouldn't have. It happens. Your parents can get past this."

"I don't think so," Perry said flatly. "Look at the first photos, of the two of them in the restaurant."

Courtney looked. "What are you seeing that I'm not seeing?"

"My mom's face. Her body language. Don't you get it?"

Courtney gave her best friend a blank look. "Get what?"

"She's happy," Perry said. "My mother is happy."

Chapter 26

When Perry Langtree got home from her Wednesday shift, the house felt ancient and lifeless.

It wasn't the same house she'd left that morning.

Then, it had been the house of a family dealing with some issues.

Now, it was the house that was about to be cut in half and divided up between two warring sides.

Why had that horrible photographer been stalking Jade? Why did people support the businesses that profited off humiliating the same celebrities those people supposedly loved? Why did Jade have to be so careless?

Perry's arms were heavy. It took great effort to clean up the tea she'd made the night before for her father.

She tried not to think about the photographs of her mother, looking happy and kissing the guy with the dark hair. She finally stopped seeing the photographs in her mind. But only because the memory had turned into a mini movie that kept playing. She could even hear the man murmuring, and her mother's laughter.

Perry turned on the small stereo they kept in the kitchen. It was tuned to a local radio station. The DJs were talking about the scandal with Jade. According to them, the young man was an actor, not a musician, and his people were claiming he hadn't known Jade was married. His name was Dalton Deangelo, and he was one of the stars on a supernatural soap opera called *One Vamp to Love*. He sounded like an idiot. Who didn't know Jade was married?

Perry turned off the radio.

The back door opened, and Garnet walked in. His face was paler than usual. He was a good-looking kid, with the square jaw of an action hero, but he looked downright weak that day.

"Hey, buddy," Perry said. "Still not feeling so hot from eating all that junk food?"

Garnet peered into their father's office. "Where's Dad?"

"He's at work, buddy. It's only four o'clock."

Garnet shook his head. "He's not at work. I phoned him to come pick me up early from school, and he wasn't at work."

"Why did you want to leave school early?"

Garnet pouted. "I didn't want to be there."

"Why's that?" She already knew the answer, but she had to ask.

"You know why," he said angrily. "Everyone knows. Even the teachers."

"Are you talking about those trash photos with Mom in them? Everyone knows how easy it is to fake those pictures."

"I'm not a baby," Garnet said. "You don't have to lie to me."

Perry took a breath. He'd been a baby the night before when he'd refused to sleep in his own bed by himself, but okay. He had a point about being able to handle the truth about their mother.

"The pictures *might* be real," Perry said.

"Are Mom and Dad getting divorced?"

"I don't know."

"Do I have to pick which one I live with, or will I go back and forth like Kyle does?"

"Let's not get ahead of ourselves."

"What about us? We're the kids. We didn't do anything wrong." His eyes glistened, and his lower lip quivered. "Did we?"

"We didn't do anything wrong."

Garnet looked away. "This is all my fault. It's because I don't look like Dad. I started the whole thing. It's because of me."

"You *do* look like Dad. If he had black hair, it would be a lot more obvious."

"What if the DNA people lied? What if I'm someone else's son? Would I have to go live with them? Would I have to move to a different city?" He was breathing raggedly, and his lower lip was still quivering. Perry knew the verge of a meltdown when she saw it. She'd seen it at Delilah's plenty of times. What helped was a sugary soda and a box of crayons.

The Langtree family didn't keep soft drinks in the house, so Perry grabbed a coconut water for her brother.

"Ew," he said. "I don't drink those."

"What do you want? A peanut butter and jam sandwich?"

His lip stopped quivering. "With crusts on or off?"

"Your choice."

"I want the round side but not the square sides."

"Deal." She started making him the sandwich.

"I do look like Dad," Garnet said. "Except for my hair. Is it possible for someone to have two dads?"

"Not in the way you're thinking," Perry said.

Garnet licked his lips and watched her make the sandwich.

"Kyle says it's okay to have divorced parents. You get to have everything twice. Christmas and other stuff." He grabbed the coconut water he had previously rejected and slurped back half the container. "Gross." He burped and wiped his mouth with the back of his hand.

"Mom and Dad both love you, no matter what," Perry said.

"Duh."

She finished making the sandwich. He took it, along with the cut-off crusts, which he ate first.

Then he came around the counter and head-butted her in the solar plexus.

"Oof," she said. "Why'd you—"

He wrapped his arms around her and hugged her.

She patted his back. "There, there, little monkey."

He burped again, then released her and went back to eating his sandwich.

When the sandwich was gone, he asked, "What's for dinner?"

"I'll have to check the binder."

Garnet went over to the binder for the first time ever and flipped it open. "Does Mom have a recipe for pizza?"

"Yes, but it's only for the weekend."

"Why?"

"I don't know."

"If I help you, can we make pizza tonight? I think Dad would like to eat pizza. Everyone likes pizza if they've had a bad day."

"Sure. Why not?" She started pulling out the ingredients to make pizza.

Garnet hummed happily to himself as he grated mozzarella cheese. He was a simple kid, and that was a good thing.

Perry, however, wasn't feeling any better.

She checked her phone. There was nothing from Dale Langtree.

Garnet and Perry finished the preparation and put the pizza in the oven.

They still hadn't heard from their father. Perry had been feeling bad, and now she felt worse. Her chest was heavy with a sense of impending doom.

Her father wasn't answering his phone, and the people he worked with didn't know where he was.

The pizza was ready.

The Langtree kids ate it alone. Dale Langtree was still missing.

At eight o'clock, Perry sent a text message to a friend, asking for advice. What she really wanted was comfort and reassurance, like what she had provided for her younger brother, but she phrased it in the form of a question.

The friend, Yaro Banks, replied that he would come over so they could talk about it in person.

Chapter 27

At eight o'clock, Yaro Banks showed up in the yellow Range Rover. He'd brought his sister, Sunshine Banks. Sunshine had refreshed the blue dye in her hair and looked stunning.

Yaro hadn't been inside the house before, so Perry offered the Banks siblings a tour.

Before they could answer, Garnet grabbed Sunshine's hand and pulled her away. "You gotta see my room," he said. "Have you ever seen a room with black walls and stars on the ceiling?"

"I have not," Sunshine said, going along with him.

Garnet chattered excitedly as he led her up the stairs.

"Love at first sight," Perry said.

Yaro said, "This always happens. People fall in love with my sister the instant they meet her."

"I noticed that. When she came to Delilah's yesterday, the kitchen staff could barely get anything done because they were too busy staring at her."

"I don't see what the fuss is about, but I am her brother."

"You're immune," Perry said.

"How old is your brother?"

"He's fifteen going on eight," she said.

"Learning issues?"

"Not that. Maybe? I don't know. Since my mother left me in charge, I swear he's regressing."

"Getting older isn't a linear process," Yaro said.

"It's not?"

Yaro scanned the living room room. "Well, technically getting older is linear, but I mean the maturity part. Sometimes I feel like I'm going on eight myself." His gaze stopped on the glass-doored cabinet next to the fireplace. "Are those Grammy awards?"

"Ugh. I wish she'd keep them somewhere private, like in her office, or down in the basement. It's so embarrassing."

Yaro walked over to the cabinet. "Nah. It's cool." He pressed his forehead to the glass, looking in. "They're bigger than you'd think. Are they heavy?"

"It's not locked. Go ahead."

Yaro opened the cabinet and took out a glass pyramid. He cleared his throat and said, "I'd like to thank the ladies and gentleman of the Academy."

"You're thinking of the Oscars," Perry said. "That's the little gold man. Mom doesn't have any of those. You're holding an AMA."

Yaro looked down at the AMA. "Does everyone who comes to your house want to hold onto your mom's awards and make dumb speeches?"

"Yes."

He put it away. "I'm not very original."

"You're one of a kind," Perry said. "And you made me laugh."

"I didn't hear any laughter."

"I was laughing on the inside."

"You were laughing inside at me," he said. "The unoriginal loser."

She shrugged. "Whatever works. You took my mind off my mom's text message yesterday, and today you're helping me with... what was it again?"

"I have an idea, but I don't want to say. I did see some photos today."

"You saw the scandalous photos of my mother, but there's more. My father has been abducted. Nobody knows where he is."

"The aliens haven't sent a ransom message from their UFO?"

"I never told you it was aliens. Are you one of them?"

"I'm not allowed to say." He walked around the living room, stopping to look at the framed prints of the family. "Your dad looks so young," he said.

"That picture's from about a decade ago. His hair's more gray now."

Yaro leaned in close to a portrait, squinting. "You were a cute kid."

"Hey! I still am."

Yaro smiled and continued snooping around. "So, are you going to tell me what's really going on with your family?"

"I already told you. My mom's hooking up with some actor in LA, and my dad has gone AWOL."

Yaro gave her a surprised look. "He's missing? For real?"

"He didn't show up at work this morning."

"Does he drink?"

"A few beers, but nothing crazy. Do you think he's on a bender? There are a few pubs he goes to with his friends."

"We could check there."

"I don't think he'd be drinking heavily. It gives him a terrible headache, and he's not supposed to mix it with his medication."

"Love makes people do stupid things."

Perry crossed her arms. "I don't think my dad's feeling a lot of love for my mom lately."

"If you want, we can go looking for him at his usual haunts. Dads love it when their kids show up and haul them off the barstool. I know mine did before he got sober. Too bad sobriety didn't agree with him."

"I'm sorry to hear that. I didn't know."

"I don't talk about my dad much. Things are good with my mom, and my uncle is like a dad to me. He's the one with the art gallery."

"When did your parents get divorced?"

"My dad died when I was fifteen."

Perry felt her heartbeat speed up. "That's how old Garnet is. He'd be crushed if anything happened to our father." Her skin prickled with sweat.

"I'm sure your dad's fine. He missed one day of work. He'll turn up." Yaro crossed the living room and hugged her. He was so warm, like a furnace.

"He'll turn up," he repeated.

Perry pressed her face into Yaro's shoulder. She was glad she'd contacted him for the second night in a row. He really was consoling her.

Two people clattered down the stairs.

Sunshine returned with Garnet, who was talking a mile a minute about his ideal car that he was going to get after his sixteenth birthday.

Yaro pulled away from Perry and stepped back a full three full steps.

Sunshine said, "We're hungry."

Perry said to Garnet, "You just ate half a large pizza by yourself. Plus a pound of cheese before it even got in the oven."

"Tell it to my stomach," Garnet said. "I'm hungry again."

Yaro said, "I could eat."

"We could order in some food," Perry said. "I have a credit card I'm allowed to use in the event of emergencies."

"I've got a better idea," Yaro said. He looked at his sister. "Are you thinking what I'm thinking?"

Sunshine nodded.

"All-you-can-eat sushi," Yaro said.

"That's not the sort of thing you can get delivered," Perry said.

"We're going out," Yaro said.

Garnet said, "Shouldn't we wait here for when Dad gets back?"

"I've got my phone," Perry said. "If he comes home to an empty house and freaks out, it serves him right."

Garnet's eyes lit up. "Can we make it look like we were abducted?"

Perry shook her head at her little brother.

Sunshine said to her own brother, "I like the way this kid thinks. An abduction plot? He's only fifteen, too."

"He's a cute kid," Yaro said. "How much sushi can you eat, Garnet?"

"All of the sushi," Garnet said, holding his arms out wide. "All of it."

"I'd like to see that," Yaro said.

"Sushi it is," Perry said. "I'll just write a note for our dad."

Sunshine clapped her hands.

"A regular note," Perry said. "Not a ransom note."

Perry wrote the note.

The four went outside and climbed into the yellow Range Rover.

Garnet sat in the front seat and pressed every button on the dashboard while Yaro drove.

They crossed town and went to a sushi place the Langtrees had never visited before.

The staff knew the Banks siblings well, and lavished the table with attention.

They also brought over sake and didn't ask Perry for ID.

With some encouragement from the Banks siblings, Perry drank sake for the first time in her life.

Not a small amount, either.

Perry was having fun.

She was not thinking about her mom in LA, the actor with the dark hair, or where her father might be.

Chapter 28

Thursday

Marcus Philby

The Thursday morning after the news about Jade and her new man hit the gossip sites, Marcus Philby woke up in his childhood bedroom under a poster of Jade. He'd been meaning to take it down ever since meeting her daughter, but he kept forgetting. It had been on the wall so long, it was just part of the room.

He sat up and rubbed his face. He reached for his phone then decided he didn't need the stress of looking at any news. He had enough going on with school. It had been a few days since he'd consumed any sort of news, so he knew nothing about the latest scandal concerning the attractive singer on the poster next to his bed.

He got up, pulled on some clothes, and went down to the kitchen.

His father, Lance Philby, was reviewing weather data on his laptop while eating cereal.

Lance said to his son, "Why am I eating cereal? I don't even like cereal."

"Dad, nobody likes cereal," Marcus said.

Lance pushed the bowl away. "Why do people eat it?"

"Because it's in the cupboard and you don't have to cook it." Marcus stuck his hand into the open cereal box and scooped a fistful of flakes into his mouth. "And because they put lots of sugar in it."

"They do," Lance said. "Your mother's trying to kill us."

"What do you mean, *us*? I'm not the one with the big life insurance policy, Dad."

Lance picked up the cereal box and read the ingredients. "What's riboflavin?"

"I believe that's one of the B vitamins."

"Did you know that not all of the vitamins are vitamins? Vitamin D is a hormone. I don't think they should be putting hormones in our food." The TV weatherman with the dreamy blue eyes picked up his spoon and resumed eating. "It doesn't even taste good."

Marcus said, "We've both got the morning free today. Why don't we go out for breakfast?"

"Out? When we have perfectly good food at home?" Lance took another bite then dropped his spoon in the bowl and pushed it away. "Where do you want to go?"

"Delilah's is good."

"Isn't that the place with the big lineups?"

"Only on the weekend. You can slide right in on weekdays."

Lance Philby got up and dumped the mushy cereal into the compost bucket.

"I thought you weren't speaking to me," Lance said casually. "You've been giving me the silent treatment. Don't think I haven't noticed."

"I've been busy with school. That's all."

"Son, you can date whoever you want. I shouldn't have questioned your intentions last week."

"I know you were only looking out for me."

Lance shook his head. "After everything Sunshine Banks put you through, I can't help but feel protective of you. And the way Yaro has been, too. I don't know what you see in that family."

"Yaro's been my best friend for years. Dating his sister was a mistake, obviously, but I'm in a good place now."

"Your mother thinks the only reason you dated her at all was because she was the one girl Yaro wouldn't try to steal from you. Like he did with Pam, and Erica, and Laurie."

"He didn't steal those girls from me. He just happened to date them after I did."

Lance said, "Your mother and I may be old, but we're not blind. He waited a while with Laurie, but not with the other two. He stole them from under your nose, and it broke your heart."

Marcus sighed. "That's just how Yaro is. He always wants what someone else has. Besides that, he's always been a good friend."

Lance raised an eyebrow. "Besides stealing your girlfriends, he's a good friend? I'd hate to see how your enemies treat you."

"We were in junior high when that stuff happened with Pam and Erica. It was a long time ago. He's changed."

"But you're making new friends at the university, aren't you? Those are the contacts who will mean the most to you over the coming years, as you work your way up in your career. Keep making new friends and get rid of the deadwood. A boy with a paintbrush isn't going to be much use to you."

"Yes, Father," Marcus said dutifully. "I'm making career contacts like a good robot."

"Being an adult isn't all fun and games."

"Let's talk about this over some breakfast and coffee," Marcus said. "Like civilized people."

Lance patted his chest and squinted at the window. "What's it like outside? Do I need a jacket?"

"You're the weatherman," Marcus said.

"I know, but it's my day off."

Marcus shook his head. "I would tell people the truth about you, but they'd never believe it."

Lance grinned. "Thanks."

They went to the front door. Lance opted to wear a light jacket, just in case it rained. "You never know," he said.

"Unbelievable."

Lance grinned and tossed the keys for his sports car at Marcus. "You can drive the Midlife Crisis." Mrs. Philby had christened Lance's convertible the Midlife Crisis, and the name had stuck.

Chapter 29

Perry Langtree

While Marcus Philby was getting an unwanted driving lesson in the Midlife Crisis from his father, Perry Langtree was waking up with her first sake hangover.

Her bed was hot and crowded.

She kicked the person next to her.

"Garnet, you're not a baby," Perry grumbled. "Go sleep in your own bed."

The person next to her rolled over and said, "I'm not Garnet."

It was Yaro.

Yaro Banks was in her bed.

Cue the panic attack.

Chapter 30

Dale Langtree

While Marcus and his weatherman father were driving the Midlife Crisis to Delilah's for breakfast, and Perry Langtree was having a panic attack over the other occupant in her bed, Dale Langtree, the son of famous country music superstar Lana Langtree, was waking up in a police holding cell.

"Hello," Dale called out groggily. "Where's my lawyer?"

A woman in uniform came to the bars and shook her head at him. "Lawyers don't usually turn up unless you call them."

Dale sat up on the thing he'd been sleeping on. It would have been generous to call it a bed. His head was pounding.

"I need to call my lawyer," he said. "How do I do that?"

"I'm not your secretary," the woman said, and she walked away.

"Hello?"

The woman was gone.

There was laughter from another cell, from a man Dale couldn't see.

"She's my favorite," the man said.

Dale replied, "Lousy service in this establishment. Not the five-star hotel I thought I booked for myself."

The man in the next cell laughed again. "I give this place two stars," he said.

"You're generous," Dale said.

"I've seen worse," the man said. "Have you ever been to jail in Mexico before?"

Dale nearly wet his pants. "We're in Mexico?" He'd blacked out much of the previous evening, but he would have remembered crossing the border into another country. Or would he? There was a terrible pain in his right hand.

The man laughed again, then moaned. "Ouch. That hurts my head. Don't make me laugh so much, fella."

Dale asked slowly and clearly, "Sir, are we in Mexico?"

"You're in the City of Stars," the man replied. "La La Land. Hollywood. Can't you tell by all the glitz and glamour?"

Dale nearly wet his pants again, this time out of relief. Also, he really had to use the washroom.

"Oh, thank God," he said. Then he took a good look around. The sweet relief he'd felt dissipated.

Dale Langtree was not in Mexico, which was good news, but he *was* in jail, and that was not ideal.

Chapter 31

Marcus Philby enjoyed driving his father's sports car so much that he took a long detour on the way to Delilah's. He didn't want to admit it out loud, but he finally understood what his dad saw in the vehicle.

They parked and went into the restaurant. There was, as he'd promised his father, no lineup and no waiting.

They were greeted inside the door by Perry's best friend, Courtney Liu.

Courtney said, "Crossword Guy!" She did a double take at Lance. "And Lance Philby? The city's most popular weatherman?"

"Guilty as charged," Lance said, grinning.

"You're even cuter in real life," Courtney said, batting her thick row of false eyelashes.

Marcus said, "He's my dad."

"I know," Courtney said. "Perry told me." She glanced back and forth between the two of them. "I see it now. Great family resemblance. No paternity test necessary!"

Lance frowned. "What?"

Marcus elbowed his father. "They joke around about things here. It's part of the appeal."

Lance said, "As long as they don't microwave the food, I'll give it a shot."

Marcus scanned the restaurant for his favorite funny waitress. "Is Perry working today?"

"She's not here," Courtney said. "You're stuck with me, boys. Right this way." She led them over to a table on the opposite side of the restaurant from where Marcus usually sat. A couple of businessmen were sitting at his usual table by the window. They were being served by a woman with a loud, raspy laugh. Marcus had never seen the other waitress before.

He asked Courtney, "Who's that? New hire?"

"That's Rhonda," Courtney said. "Our cook, Donny, called his cousin to come fill in when Perry didn't show up this morning for her shift."

Lance Philby asked, "Who's Perry?"

His son replied, "She's my friend who works here. Her dad's an engineer with the city. I told you about her. I had dinner with her dad, remember?"

"Right. The eighteen-year-old," Lance said. He picked up the menu and studied it.

Marcus looked up at Courtney. "Is it normal for Perry to miss a shift? I hope everything's okay."

Courtney glanced around then bent down so her head was the same height as his. Quietly, she said, "Some stuff's been happening with her family. It's worse than the typical stuff. Perry's taking it hard. She sent me some crazy text messages late last night. I think she was drinking."

The older Philby man looked up from his menu and said, "If she's only eighteen, she shouldn't be drinking."

Marcus gave his father a dirty look. "Not helpful, Dad."

Courtney said, "She'll get through it. She's a tough cookie."

"What about Mr. Langtree?" Marcus asked. "How's Dale doing?"

Courtney bit her lower lip. "I'd rather not say. I don't want to be part of the whole gossip cycle, you know?"

Marcus said nothing. He wished she would.

"That's very honorable of you," Lance said. "What's the daily special?"

"You can get any of the breakfast items with a banana muffin instead of toast."

"Oh, that's a tough one," Lance said. "I do like banana muffins, but I also like toast."

Courtney gave him a slow blink. "Yeah. Life's hard," she said.

Marcus made eye contact with Courtney and mouthed the words *I'm sorry*.

"It's okay," she said softly. "I also have a dad. I get it."

The weatherman paid them no attention as he scoured the menu, his lips moving as he read the breakfast menu.

Marcus said to Courtney, "I hope Perry's okay. When you see her, let her know I'm sorry I missed her."

"Sure will, Crossword Guy. You want the usual?"

He handed her the menu. "Yes, please. With the banana muffin instead of the toast."

"Good. That's all we've got. We just ran out of toast."

He gave her a sidelong look. "Are you really out of toast?"

She winked at him. "All our bread is raw."

"That doesn't sound good."

They smiled at each other.

"Time's up," Courtney said to Lance as she yanked his menu away. "Pick something or hit the bricks."

"But I wasn't done looking," the weatherman said.

"Leave some reading for your next visit," Courtney said. "Do you want a ham and cheese omelet with a banana muffin?"

The weatherman's blue eyes lit up. "I do," he said.

"Coming right up," she said. "Rhonda's coming around with the coffee pot right now. Please keep your arms and legs within the ride at all times. You can wash your hands before you eat or after but not both, because it creates a bottleneck in the washroom."

She stepped away, and Rhonda stepped in to fill their coffee cups.

After Rhonda had walked away, Lance said, "I like this place."

"Dad, you can wash your hands before the food gets here if you want. That's just something they say."

"No need." Lance pulled out his phone and tapped the screen.

"Put that away," Marcus said. "They've got a bucket where they put confiscated phones. You'll have to pay a ransom to get it back out again."

"Charming," Lance said, continuing to use his phone. "Oh, no," he said. "Is this your friend's father?"

He turned the phone screen to show Marcus.

The headline read: *Jade's Hubby Doesn't Approve of New Squeeze.*

The article was accompanied by pictures of Dale Langtree, the conservative city engineer, punching a buff young man in front of a popular LA nightclub.

Marcus grabbed the phone from his father.

The article was from that morning. The assault had happened the night before. Dale had been arrested by the local authorities.

Lance said, "I'm glad your mother never drove me to do anything like that. We had our moments, but not like this. I'm so glad I turned down those job offers for the LA market." He sipped his coffee. "There were so *many* offers, too."

Marcus ignored his father. His head was swimming with worries about Perry. She was mature for her age, but she was still only eighteen. Her younger brother, Garnet, was fifteen, and not very mature for his age. Their mom was out of town, and their dad was in jail. The two kids were completely on their own. It wasn't a good situation. No wonder Perry hadn't shown up for work that day.

Chapter 32

Dale Langtree

Dale was curled up on the hard platform in his cell, truly feeling sorry for himself, when a pair of glittering, rhinestone-studded cowgirl boots came into view on the other side of the bars.

"Dale Joshua Harley Junior," a woman said.

Dale jerked upright. "Mom?"

Country superstar legend Lana Langtree stood on the other side of the bars, her arms crossed over a dress that was as dazzling as her white boots. Dale was glad to see his famous mother, but the outfit stung his eyes.

Dale stammered, "Wha-what are you doing here?"

"Don't you know, darlin'? The one thing every mother dreams of is seein' her precious son locked up in a jail cell." She scoffed. "Why do you think I'm here, Dale? I'm hauling your butt out of here before you get yourself in deeper trouble. What were you thinking? Punching a man in the face while people took pictures?"

"He started it," Dale said. "I only wanted to talk to my wife."

"At least you didn't punch her."

"Mother! I would never!"

"I'm not sure I would have had as much self-restraint," the blond superstar said. "The nerve of that woman! Running around with some young wannabe while her sweet little babies are at home all alone."

Dale didn't say anything. His mother could have been describing herself.

"It sounds exactly like the things I did when you were little, Dale, and I deeply regret those things,"

Lana Langtree said. "If I'd done a better job raising you kids, I might not have to jump on so many overnight flights to bail you kids out of jail."

Dale got up from the uncomfortable platform. His head swam with stars, but he made it over to the bars without fainting.

"You posted bail?"

His mother shook his head. "No need. They're dropping the charges."

Dale didn't bother asking how she'd made that happen. Lana Langtree was like a freight train—a pretty, sweet-talking, rhinestone-covered freight train. People got out of her way and then thanked her for passing through.

"That's a relief," he said.

"You're welcome."

"Thank you," he said belatedly. "I owe you."

"Have you even called Peridot and Garnet? The children must be worried sick about you."

"They're fine," he said. "I haven't talked to them, but I left a note on the television. Or the refrigerator." He scratched his head. "Or did I? Doesn't matter. Perry's a smart girl."

"Smarter than you, Dale Joshua Harley Junior."

Dale swallowed hard. "Perry has been doing a great job filling in for Jade. She's very responsible."

"Unlike you, Dale Joshua Harley Junior. Where did you get the idea of flying into town and punching people you don't like? Must have been your father's influence."

Dale knew to stay quiet. He'd learned it from his mother. Lana Langtree had seen her share of trouble over the years, but at least she'd cleaned up her act before the era of cell phone cameras being everywhere.

Lana turned around, casting rhinestone sparkles through the jail. "Where's the staff when you need them?"

"Mother, please don't call them *the staff*."

"Whoever they are, they need to get you out of here." She tapped the bars. "I may be tougher than nails, but I can't bend metal bars." She put her fingers in her mouth and whistled for some assistance. "A little help checking out of this fine establishment, please?"

A woman in uniform came running, keys jingling.

Chapter 33

Marcus Philby

Marcus fidgeted restlessly while his father, who'd finished his own hash browns, moved on to picking them off Marcus's plate.

The weatherman said, "Why am I eating these? I don't even like potatoes."

"It's because they're salty," Marcus said.

"Oh. Right." Lance stabbed more hash browns.

"Dad, do you have anywhere you need to be this morning?"

"Nowhere important. I'm having a nice day with my son. We should do this more often. I wish you'd take that internship at the station. We could see each other all the time."

Marcus buttoned his lightweight plaid jacket then unbuttoned it.

"Something's bothering you," Lance said. "Did you want to talk about it?"

Marcus surprised himself with the words that came out of his mouth. "I'm not sure I want to go to school to be an engineer."

Lance slowly chewed on hash browns then washed them down with coffee. "But you've been talking about it ever since you were ten. You wanted to build bridges."

"Of course I did. I was a little kid. Little kids want to build bridges, and fly to the moon. They don't know the reality behind those storybook jobs."

Lance nodded. "People always think being a weatherman is so easy."

Marcus wasn't surprised his father was turning the conversation focus onto himself.

"But enough about me," Lance said. "I'm here for you. Being a weatherman is my number-two job. My number-one job is being married to your mother and raising my son."

Marcus was so surprised by his father's attention, he found himself speechless.

"I've been thinking about that night we talked about your friend, the waitress," Lance said. "I wish I could take back what I said. I know I said it already, but I'm not sure you heard me. You really should date whoever you want." He pointed his fork at his son. "As long as she's eighteen or older."

"I know you were just looking out for me."

"Someone has to. Your friends all have their own agendas. I'm a dad. All I want is what's best for my son." He grabbed Marcus's plate and set it on top of his empty plate for easier access to the hash browns. "I'm glad we're having this time together, and not just because this food is so much better than cereal."

"Me, too."

"Are you going to drop out of school and take the internship?"

Marcus swallowed hard. It was hard to give in to his father's wishes, even if they were in alignment with what Marcus wanted. It was hard to reverse course on the career path he'd been talking about for over a decade.

"I'll finish up the year," Marcus said. "In case things don't work out and I want to go back."

"Smart boy." Lance Philby managed to not gloat, which made the whole thing a bit easier for Marcus.

"And I'm only taking the internship because I love being at the studio," Marcus said. "Not because it was your idea."

"Of course." A tiny bit of gloating crept out the corner of Lance Philby's mouth.

"And I'm going to work hard. If I don't work twice as hard as the other interns, I want them to fire me. No special treatment just because I'm your son."

"Fair enough."

The other waitress, Rhonda, came by with more coffee. With her gravelly voice that made her sound much older than she looked, Rhonda said, "Are my eyes deceiving me, or are you two boys having a special moment in spite of the food, the music, and the decor?"

"We may be," Lance Philby said, beaming.

After Rhonda left, Marcus said, "Since you don't have any plans this morning, I wouldn't mind stopping by to check on a friend. I'll just be a minute. You can wait in the car."

"Is this your friend the eighteen-year-old waitress who didn't show up for work today?"

Marcus looked down, his cheeks flushing. "Yes. Stop calling her that. Her name is Perry."

"I'll go with you, but I'm not waiting in the car. I need to meet this special young woman who has turned your whole world upside down."

"Sure," Marcus said. "You can meet her."

Lance Philby finished his coffee and got up. "Now, if you'll excuse me, I'm going to find out where my phone is being held for ransom and pay whatever fee it is they demand."

"The funds go to a good charity," Marcus said.

"I'm sure they do," Lance said, smiling.

Chapter 34

Perry pulled away so quickly from the young man sharing her bed that she fell right out of bed, onto the floor.

"I thought you were my brother," she said. "What are you doing in here?"

Yaro yawned and rubbed his face. He was shirtless. The rest of him was under the blankets.

"I *was* sleeping, until you started kicking me," he said.

"Why? Why are you sleeping in my bed?"

"Don't you remember? Last night when we got back here from the restaurant, you said we should all put on pajamas."

Perry looked down at herself. She was wearing flannel pajamas. Top and bottoms.

"But you're not wearing pajamas," she said.

"Oh, but I am." Yaro flung back the blankets. He was wearing a pair of Perry's pajama bottoms. They were small, and way too short for his long legs.

Memories from the night before came back to Perry in flashes. She recalled the four of them laughing all the way home from the restaurant, then using the family's professional-quality karaoke system. They'd been singing until the wee hours of the morning. Sunshine Banks had dressed up in one of Jade's fancy dresses that had been worn to an awards show. Garnet fell asleep with his head in Sunshine's lap.

Yaro swung his legs out of the bed and stood up. "If I'm making you uncomfortable like this, I'll go put my regular clothes on."

"Do that," she said.

He stood there. "But you have seen me naked before."

"Last night?"

"No. At the community center." He rubbed his stomach and yawned.

"Yaro, did we have sex last night?" She made a twirling motion with her finger. "With each other?"

"No," he said. "We didn't even kiss."

"Are you sure?"

He held up both hands. "I'm not gonna lie. I thought about it, but you were drunk, and I'm not that guy."

"Oh."

"Plus you kept talking about someone named Toph, and how you were going to rock his world in the walk-in cooler. Honestly, I found it to be a turn-off."

"Good," she said.

"But you're sober now," he said, taking a step toward her.

Perry breathed into her hand and sniffed it. "Don't be so sure of that. What did we drink after the sake?"

"I had one of your dad's beers. You had a couple. I should have been watching you more closely. Sometimes I forget how young you are."

He took another step closer.

The doorbell for the front door rang.

Yaro turned his head. "Someone's at the door."

Perry darted around him, ran out of her bedroom, and ran for the front door.

"Daddy?"

She yanked open the front door.

The person ringing the bell was not her father. Why would she have thought that? Dale Langtree would have used his key.

Standing in the doorway were two men. One of them was the city's most popular weatherman. The other was Crossword Guy.

Chapter 35

Marcus Philby

Marcus heard shuffling inside the home.

His father said, "Nice house. New build or renovation?"

Before Marcus could answer, the door to the Langtree house swung open.

Perry Langtree stood in the doorway in a mismatched pair of flannel pajamas. Her hair was a mess. *A cute mess*, Marcus thought. An *adorable* mess. Why had he not kissed her yet?

Perry blinked at him. "You're not my dad," she said.

"I'm not," Marcus said. "Do you know where he is?"

"What kind of game is this?" Perry leaned out and peered around him. "Is he here with you?"

"No," Marcus said.

Perry pointed at Marcus's father, Lance Philby, who was standing a few feet back on the walkway. "You brought my favorite weatherman," she said. "Why? What are you doing here? Did Yaro and Sunshine phone you?"

Marcus looked down at his feet. He couldn't bear to look into her eyes as he broke the news to her.

"Perry, your father is in Los Angeles," he said. "He punched someone last night, and he was arrested by the police."

She snorted. "That does not sound like something Dale Langtree would do."

Lance Philby jumped into the conversation. "Love makes people do crazy things," he said. "I'm sure your dad didn't mean to get arrested."

Perry shook her head. "Why do you keep saying he was arrested?"

"Because he was," Marcus said. "Do you want to see the photos?"

Perry tugged at her pajamas and cast her eyes down. "I don't need to," she said glumly. "I believe you. That does explain why he's not here."

"Has your father ever done anything like this?"

"No. It's not like my dad to fly to another city and punch someone, but it does sound like something my grandma would do. Maybe she gave him the idea."

Lance Philby said, "By your grandma, do you mean—"

Marcus elbowed his father to be quiet. Now was not the time.

Perry said, "Thanks for the, um, telegram or whatever this is. I guess I'll... I don't know what I'll do. My mom didn't put anything about a situation like this in the binder."

Marcus asked, "How's Garnet? How are you guys doing?"

Perry winced and took a breath high in her chest.

There was the sound of laughter inside the Langtree house. Marcus jerked his head back. It was familiar laughter.

Marcus asked, "Does your brother have friends over?"

"Sort of. New friends." Perry stepped outside of the house and closed the door behind her. "It was nice of you to come by."

"How's your brother going to take the news?"

"Garnet's okay as long as I feed him regularly and keep him distracted. We'll deal with it." She kept her gaze down, avoiding eye contact with Marcus.

Marcus followed her gaze to a couple of empty beer bottles at the edge of the front step. "What's this?" He tapped a bottle with his shoe. "Did you have a house party last night?"

"Kind of," she said.

Lance interjected, "Miss, if there are people in your house that you'd rather not have in there, just say the word. I'm sure your dad wouldn't want people here taking advantage of you."

Perry looked up at Marcus, her eyes brimming with tears. "I'm sorry," she said.

"You don't have to apologize to me," Marcus said, pulling his head back. "I should apologize for coming over here unannounced. I should have gotten your phone number from Courtney instead of charging over here like some sort of..."

"Knight," Perry said. "Like some sort of heroic knight."

Marcus grinned. "That's me, all right. Only instead of a horse, I'm riding a Midlife Crisis." He gestured to his dad's sports car.

"Nice wheels," Perry said.

Lance, the proud owner of the sports car, said, "Thank you. When your father gets back to town, maybe we can all go shopping for cars. Buying a car can be just as satisfying as punching some young punk in the face, and it lasts longer."

Perry chortled. "Your dad's funny in real life," she said to Marcus.

Marcus replied, "I'm glad you find him worthy of the shrine you made for him in the attic."

Lance raised his hand. "Excuse me? What shrine?"

Perry and Marcus shared a smile.

Marcus said, "Since you're already playing hooky from work, do you want to hang out with us today?"

"Hang out with you and your dad?"

"Why not? I hung out with your dad." He buttoned his flannel jacket nervously. "Garnet can come, too, obviously. If you're letting him skip the whole school day. We could go to the Pier, or we could go see a movie."

Lance said, "That does sound fun. Can we get ice cream at the Pier?"

Marcus shook his head and said to Perry, "I just fed him breakfast. Can you believe it? Asking for ice cream already?"

"He's exactly like Garnet," Perry said. "A bottomless pit for food." She picked up the beer bottles and pressed her back against the door without opening it. "Can you guys wait out here for a few minutes while I take care of some things in here?"

"Sure," Marcus said.

Lance, who'd turned and was looking down the street, said to his son, "Look at that yellow Range Rover. It's like the one your friend Yaro drives around. How many of those do you suppose are in this city?"

"I don't know, Dad. Not many. That's why..." Marcus trailed off. He looked at the yellow truck then at Perry.

Perry shrank back against the door and chewed her lower lip. She looked down.

Marcus took a step back. "He's here, isn't he?"

Perry nodded. "With Sunshine. His sister. They're both here."

Marcus took another step back. "You're wearing pajamas."

"I just woke up. They both stayed over. Nothing happened, Marcus. I'm just friends with Yaro."

Lance Philby made a sound but managed to keep his mouth shut.

"You're eighteen," Marcus said. "You're a bit old for sleepovers with friends." He turned away from her, his face burning and his fists clenching.

"Wait," she said.

Marcus kept turning so he didn't have to see her face.

It didn't matter what she was going to say next. He'd heard it so many times before. She was "only friends" with Yaro. He was "such a good listener." He was around when Marcus wasn't. Yaro only wanted the best for his friends, but he had feelings, too, and sometimes he acted on them, but "he'd never meant to."

Marcus walked toward his father's car, but all he could see was the glare of the yellow Range Rover down the street.

He was dimly aware of his father giving Perry a card with his phone number. "I'm sure your dad would do the same for my son if the roles were reversed," Lance Philby said. "Please call us if you need help with anything."

"Thanks for coming by," Perry said. "It was very nice of you. Nicer than I deserve."

"Don't say that, young lady. You're not the first girl to get bamboozled by the Banks family, and you won't be the last. I wish we were meeting under better circumstances. I'm sure we'll see each other again."

"I don't know about that," she said.

"Keep your chin up," Lance said. "Your family needs you to be strong now."

"I'm trying," Perry said.

"That's all you can do," Lance said. "We'll talk again soon."

Marcus yelled for his dad to get going already.

He slid into the passenger side of the car and slammed the door.

Chapter 36

Perry Langtree slunk back into her house feeling, to borrow her grandmother's term, "lower than a toad's belly."

The hangover had been bad enough, but then the shame kicked in. She was sick to her stomach, sweating through her pajamas, and her hands and feet were tingling.

She walked to the bathroom on shaky legs, where she trembled all over as she splashed cold water on her face.

She could hear Sunshine, Garnet, and Yaro in the kitchen, laughing and having a good time.

Yaro knocked on the bathroom door. "Come and join us for some pancakes! Sunshine found all the ingredients plus chocolate chips."

"I'll be out in a minute."

"Are you okay? You didn't drink that much, Perry. You shouldn't have much more than a headache."

She yanked the door open. "I thought you weren't keeping track of how much I was drinking?"

He gave her a startled look. "I wasn't, but it was only sake and then beer. We weren't doing shots. How bad could it be?"

"It's pretty bad," she said.

"Pancakes will make it all better," he said, smiling.

"No pancakes," she said.

"Suit yourself. More for the rest of us."

He went back to the kitchen without another word.

For the next two hours, Perry stuck to the sidelines, trying to fade into the background.

On the plus side, Sunshine and Yaro did a great job of keeping Garnet entertained.

Perry used the time to make some calls and figure out what was happening with their father.

She learned that Jade had checked herself into a private wellness center—or so her personal assistant claimed.

Dale Langtree was not currently in jail and didn't have any pending charges.

He was on his way home, and Perry's grandmother wished she could come up and visit, but she had to get back to her tour. Missing a show would mean millions of dollars lost and would affect countless people, not to mention the disappointed fans.

Perry finally spoke to her father from a pay phone. He'd lost his phone during a fight with some paparazzi.

"I'll be home tomorrow morning," he said. "About ten o'clock."

"Good. I'll be at work, and Garnet will be at school. We'll see you back home for dinner."

"That's it?"

"What do you want from me? A lecture?"

"How about some congratulations? You're the one who wanted me to take action in my life instead of complaining about it."

"Dad, I didn't tell you to fly to LA and start punching people."

There was a pause. Perry pictured her dad grinning. There was a lightness to his voice as he said, "I think you did tell me to do that. Between the lines."

"Are you smiling, Dad? Are you actually happy about all of this?"

"In a way, yes. I am smiling. I don't know why."

"I know why," she said. "It's because this is exactly what you've always wanted to do."

"You may be right. You're very wise for a kid."

"If I'm so wise, why is my life a disaster?"

"Because you're only eighteen. It won't get straightened out for another thirty or so years."

"Thanks."

"It might take longer. I don't know. I haven't gotten there yet myself."

"Did Grandma really show up at the jail in one of her stage costumes?"

Dale chuckled. "She sure did. Honestly, it was worth spending a night in jail to see that."

"Don't do it again. Promise you'll come right home?"

"I will. What's for dinner tomorrow night?"

"I haven't checked the binder."

"Perry, you have my permission to throw the binder away. Forget about all your mother's instructions. Make whatever you want."

She thanked him, told him to stay away from the press, and ended the call.

Chapter 37

Friday

Courtney Liu didn't have a shift at Delilah's on Friday, but she came in before opening to talk to Perry.

Perry Langtree explained everything that had happened on Wednesday, from dinner and sake at the all-you-can-eat sushi place, to beer and karaoke at her house, and then waking up on Thursday with Yaro Banks in her bed. She hadn't gotten to the part about Marcus showing up with his father when Courtney got angry.

Courtney's nostrils flared. "Did Yaro Banks storm your castle?"

"No," Perry said. "He didn't even broach the moat."

"Are you sure?"

"It's fuzzy, but I remember most of the evening. It was my idea for us to put on pajamas, plus Garnet was in my bed with us most of the night. I have pictures on my phone of the three of us eating late-night popcorn and putting pieces in Garnet's nose."

Courtney started filling the salt shakers.

"You don't have to do that," Perry said. "Maggie will be here any minute. She can fill the salt shakers."

"I have to do something," Courtney said. "If I don't keep moving, I'm going to cry." Her lower lip trembled. "I'm sorry. I'm a bad friend. I can't believe I'm getting upset about my life when yours is falling apart."

"You can be upset about whatever you want to be upset about."

"Can you believe I actually liked Yaro?"

"Don't let this whole thing stop you from whatever you've got going on with him. Honestly. Don't give up on something just because things might be awkward around me."

"I don't want him," Courtney said. "And stop putting some of your tips in my jar. I don't want your pity tips."

"Okay." Perry gathered the rest of the salt shakers and started unscrewing the caps.

Courtney looked up at her friend. "You look really sad. If you don't want to work today because you're sad about your parents, I can trade shifts."

"I'm actually feeling sad about Marcus," Perry said.

Courtney brightened up. "I forgot to tell you! Crossword Guy came in yesterday with his dad, the weatherman. They were adorable together. You have to meet his dad. He's so funny. I confiscated his cell phone for ransom, and he loved it."

"I met him already," Perry said. "They came to the house after they had breakfast."

"Your house?"

Perry nodded. She could barely get the words out. "Marcus saw Yaro's truck out front and figured out he was there."

Courtney dropped the salt. "Did you explain what happened? That it wasn't what it looked like?"

"I tried."

"He didn't believe you?"

"Can you blame him?"

Courtney looked down. "I guess not."

"You should have seen his face," Perry said. "The way he looked at me." She clenched her jaw.

Courtney hugged her friend. "Those two have history," she said softly. She patted Perry's back. "Yaro told me he always liked Marcus's girlfriends too much. He told me he was trying to change his ways."

"I feel so bad," Perry said, holding back sobs. "I hurt all over. Can a person have a hangover for two days?"

"It's not a hangover," Courtney said, squeezing her tighter.

"I don't want to feel like this."

"It's okay to feel bad sometimes."

"But it feels like there's a knife in my chest. Something's physically wrong with me. Do you think feeling sad like this can give you organ damage?"

Courtney pulled back and looked her best friend in the eyes. "Your parents are splitting up. The guy you like thinks you slept with his best friend. I know things are pretty dark right now, but it'll get better."

"That's not the worst of it," Perry said.

"There's more?"

Perry nodded. Very solemnly, she said, "If I can't find someone to kiss me before the summer solstice, I have to make out with Toph."

Courtney took in a deep breath. With equal solemnity, she said, "I know someone who does fake IDs. We can get one for you then smuggle you out of the country."

"That seems reasonable."

"I'll use the cell phone ransom money to buy you a whole new identity."

"That's great and everything, but I could never leave you, Courtney. You're my best friend."

Courtney grinned. "That's why I'll be going with you."

"We can afford that?"

"The ransom business has been good lately."

Chapter 38

When Perry got home from her shift at Delilah's, she was surprised to find her father in the kitchen, chopping vegetables. She'd known he would be getting home that day, but seeing him cooking was a shocker. He was wearing an apron.

"Wow," Perry said. "The whole house smells like roast beef."

"I'm making brisket," Dale Langtree said. "It's one of my mother's recipes." He nodded at the cookbook that was open on the counter. The photo showed the famous country superstar posing behind a full dinner table in a rhinestone-studded apron.

Perry snorted. "You mean it's one of Lana Langtree's famous down-home recipes that you can't remember her serving even one time when you were growing up? How much did the publisher pay those ghostwriters?"

Dale chuckled. "Not enough. They're good recipes."

"It does smell good. How was your flight?"

"It got me home, and that's all that matters."

"Did you find your phone?"

"Bought a new one. I got some things for you kids, too." He nodded at a pile of brand-new electronic devices, still in their boxes.

"Gosh, Dad. Overcompensate much?"

"I've still got the receipts, Peridot. I can take it all back to the store."

"Strike my sassy comments from the record," Perry said. "I love it when you overcompensate."

Dale smiled and continued chopping celery.

Perry stole a piece and crunched it. "When's Mom getting out of rehab?"

"She's not in rehab."

"Right. She just checked into a spa that has no drugs or alcohol and a bunch of counselors. What's she getting treated for, anyway? Being a massive—"

"That's her business," he said, cutting her off. After a moment of chopping, he said, "It's a sex and love addiction program."

"Is that a real thing?"

"I'm told it is."

"Do you think it's hereditary?"

Dale stopped chopping and gave his daughter a wary look. "Is there something you want to talk about?"

"Not with my dad."

"Why not? He's the only one around. Plus he's pretty worldly, now that he's spent a night in the clink."

"Okay," she said. "You remember Marcus, right?"

"The young man who wasn't sure if engineering was the career for him? Nice kid. How's it going with him?"

"Not great," Perry said, and she explained everything that had happened.

Dale Langtree was visibly rattled by the part about Yaro being in Perry's bedroom, but he got through it.

"Perry, that's a tough one," he said. "But I think what matters the most—what always matters most—is that you're honest with yourself as much as you are with him."

"I'm trying," she said.

He nodded then frowned. "Can I tell you something? It's probably going to come out sooner or later, but I need to get ahead of it."

"Sure," she said.

He paused, and the mood in the kitchen changed. Perry's heart rate sped up.

"Garnet isn't my son," he said.

Perry felt hot tears flood her eyes. She managed to hold them back, but only barely.

"I lied," he said. "I lied about the paternity test results. It was the only thing I could do to try to keep this family together." He looked down. "It bought us a few more years, and that's the important part to remember. I stand by what I did. If I could turn back time, I wouldn't have sent in the samples in the first place, but I did. And then, after that, I did what I thought I had to."

A long, awful moment passed.

Perry asked, "Does Garnet know?"

"Not yet. Can you help me tell him?" He waved a hand. "Forget I asked. You don't need to get dragged down with me. I'll tell him myself."

"We might not have to tell him at all. I hate keeping things from him, but I can probably keep a secret as big as this."

"I can't ask you to do that. Also, I have a feeling that once your mother and I get going with the divorce, things are going to come out whether we want them to or not."

"Was it... the guy? The one you punched?"

"No. He's a new one. There have been a lot of new ones."

Perry lost it. She swore, and then she called her mother the bad word she'd been prevented from saying before.

Dale didn't argue.

Perry said, "Is there anything else I should know about? Tell it to me straight."

"On my end? No. That's it. I don't know about your mother."

Perry sniffed and composed herself.

"You're not very surprised," he said.

She looked away. "On some level, maybe I always knew."

"Was it the black hair?"

Perry frowned. "Maybe it was all the 'fruit of my loins' talk. You really did lay it on thick." She took another piece of celery. "Did you ever...?" She couldn't even ask the question.

"You're mine," he said. "You're a Langtree, through and through."

"Are you just saying that, or did you actually have me tested?"

"Your grandmother insisted on it. Remember when you and your brother came to my office to give blood for a blood drive? That was for DNA testing."

"Sneaky," Perry said.

"We double-checked Garnet, too. Then my mother had her lawyers change her will to specifically include Garnet as a full grandchild, regardless of any evidence that might come to light in the future."

Perry shivered, even though the kitchen was warm. It felt lousy to be grateful to have something her brother didn't.

"He's still ours," Dale said. "Garnet is your brother, and he'll always be my son, no matter how he came into our lives."

"You say that now, when he's fifteen and adorable. How are you going to feel when he's nineteen and he's getting in trouble? You might want to disown him then."

"He'll be fine. He's got an amazing big sister to help him stick to the right path."

"I'm not sure I'm the best role model. I can be pretty stupid sometimes. What if something had happened to him when I was drunk?"

"Let's not worry about that. You did the best you could under difficult circumstances, and it's not going to happen again."

Perry looked over at the pile of electronics. "That doesn't seem like enough now. I feel like we should get more stuff for Garnet to make up for what he'll have to go through."

"I could get more stuff. The store's still open a few more hours."

"But that's not right. You can't buy away people's pain."

"You really can't," Dale said. "Welcome to being a parent." He came around the counter and hugged her. She'd been getting a lot of hugs that day, and she'd needed every one of them. "You've done a great job helping out. I mean it."

"Better than you," she said. "I didn't punch anyone, or get arrested."

He patted her back. "Things will work out with you and Marcus. I've got a good feeling about that guy."

Chapter 39

Saturday

When Perry took her meal break on Saturday, Donny made her a special breakfast with fried eggs and bacon arranged in a happy face.

"That was tougher than it looked," Donny said. "All the bacon kept coming out straight. I went through three bags until I got the shape just right."

Perry took the breakfast, sat on a pickle bucket, and picked at her food.

Donny said, "We're all sorry about what's happening with your family. What can we do to help?"

"Stop being so nice to me," Perry said. "I just want things to go back to normal."

"Okay," Donny said, and he took back the bacon.

"That's better," Perry said.

Toph came over and shoved both of the eggs into his mouth.

"Perfect," Perry said. "Except I am hungry."

Donny handed her his silicon tongs. "Here. Help yourself to whatever's in the burn tray." The burn tray was where Donny threw everything that had gotten burned, was the wrong item, or didn't turn out right for various reasons.

Perry happily dug through for random bits of charred meat to fill her plate.

Toph asked, "Is it true? Is Jade divorcing your dad?"

"It's mutual," Perry said. "And I think it will be better for both of them in the end."

"My parents got divorced last year," Toph said. "The first thing they told me was that it wasn't going to change anything for me." He laughed hollowly. "Lie number one."

"I'm sorry to hear that," Perry said. "I had no idea."

"They said they spent my college fund on lawyer fees, but, just between us, I don't think there ever was any college fund."

Perry offered Toph her plate. "Have some burned meat."

"Thanks." He took a bite. "When is your friend Sunshine going to come back?"

"I don't think we'll see her around here. She came over to my house, and she went through a bunch of my mom's stuff without permission. I may have told her I never wanted to see her again."

Toph gave her a surprised look. "It must be hard being you." He waved one hand. "With your family stuff. My family's got problems, but they're just regular problems."

"I'm sorry about your parents splitting up," Perry said. "If you ever want someone to talk to, I'm here."

"You got a lot nicer after you changed your hair," Toph said. "No offence, but when I first started here, I almost quit the first day because of you."

"But I'm still the exact same person."

"No. My mom's a hairdresser. She says that people only make big changes to their hair when they don't feel like they're the same person they used to be."

Donny came over to where Toph and Perry were sitting. The two younger employees looked up at him for words of wisdom.

"Shovel that food down faster," he said. "Break time's almost over, chuckle bunnies."

Toph said to Perry, "That's his new insult. Chuckle bunnies. I don't even know what it means."

"Let's go, let's go," Donny said. He grabbed the last piece of charred sausage from Perry's plate—the perfect one she'd been saving for her last bite—and stuffed it in his mouth.

Perry smiled. Her family was going through a hard time, and she'd ruined things with Marcus, but at least things were normal at work.

Chapter 40

Monday

Perry Langtree didn't know what Monday had in store for her, but she was absolutely certain that Marcus Philby wouldn't be coming in for his usual breakfast.

That was why, when Courtney Liu said, "Crossword Guy is here," Perry rolled her eyes.

"Don't make that face," Courtney said. "Do you want to wait on him, or would it be too awkward? I could take his table if you want. It's not busy yet."

Perry leaned over, looked past her best friend, and saw that Crossword Guy really was there. With his newspaper and pen in hand.

Perry froze. "What do I say?"

Courtney took Perry's hand and placed it on the handle of the coffee pot. "Start with coffee," she said.

Perry brought the coffee pot over and filled Marcus's cup halfway.

Marcus looked at the half-full cup then up at Perry. "Is that how it's going to be now?"

Perry added a little more coffee.

"I guess slightly over half-full is a good start," Marcus said.

"A good start for what?"

"For us being friends."

She blinked at him. Something had to be said, and it seemed awfully early in the morning for the subject, but she broached it anyway.

"I didn't sleep with Yaro," Perry said.

Marcus frowned. "He told me he wore your pajamas and slept in your bed. There are photos."

"You know what I mean," she said. "I didn't *sleep with* him."

"That's your business and his," Marcus said. "It's not my business."

"It's not? But he's your best friend, and I'm... your favorite waitress."

"I'm not so sure about that." Marcus pursed his lips. "Yaro's not my best friend anymore." He didn't comment on who his favorite waitress might or might not be. "We may not be friends anymore at all."

"I'm sorry to hear that."

"It was a long time coming. When you get to be the ripe old age of twenty-one, you'll understand. People can outgrow each other."

"But you guys got along so well. You had your special handshake."

"I'm okay. I have my hands full as it is. I don't need to concern myself with other people's love lives." He unfolded the newspaper.

"Really? It's just that you seemed upset when you came by my house on Thursday morning and found out he was there."

"I was upset," he said. "But I had no right to be. You are your own person, and your life is complicated." He uncapped his pen. "May I have the basic breakfast this morning, or is the kitchen out of eggs?"

"What kind of a question is that? What kind of restaurant would run out of eggs?"

Marcus kept a straight face.

"We've got everything," Perry said. "Even eggs."

"Great. I'm looking forward to it." He gave her a quick smile then began reading the clues for his puzzle.

Perry wandered back to the waitress station, feeling dazed. She punched in the order while Courtney hovered impatiently, waiting to hear how it had gone.

Courtney crossed her arms and tapped her foot. "Well?"

"He wants to be friends. That's what he said, more or less."

"How do you feel about that?"

"Surprised, mostly. I thought I'd never see him again." Perry glanced over at Crossword Guy then back at Courtney. "He's really into his routine. That's the only reason he's here. Maybe I should switch off of Mondays."

"There are plenty of places a person can go for toast and poached eggs," Courtney said. "If he didn't want to see you, he would have gone somewhere else."

Perry wasn't so sure of that. She wondered if Marcus might have a form of OCD that caused him to visit the same restaurant every Monday morning no matter how much he hated the waitress.

More customers came in and the place started to fill up.

For the duration of Marcus's visit, Perry was reasonably polite but only filled his coffee cup half full on the refills.

He left his usual tip and left when her back was turned.

Chapter 41

Crossword Guy showed up at his usual time, newspaper in hand.

Perry filled his coffee cup slightly over halfway.

"That's perfect," he said. "I'm trying to cut down anyway."

"The usual?"

"Unless you're out of eggs."

"We just got some new chickens."

"You keep those chickens in the kitchen?"

"They're good company for the cow."

"Excellent." Marcus uncapped his pen and looked down at his crossword puzzle.

"Is that everything for you, sir?"

He glanced up. "How are things going with your family?"

"Could be worse," Perry said. "My mother is still at the treatment center. Her lawyer sent my father an offer. He refused."

"Dale is a smart man," Marcus said. "You never take the first offer."

"You don't?"

"Everyone knows that."

"I didn't know that."

Marcus picked up his coffee and took a sip. "Whatever happens, I hope things don't get bad for you and your brother. How's Garnet doing?"

"Surprisingly well. He got some bad news, but he's dealing with it. Our cookie budget is through the roof, though."

Marcus chuckled. "Could be worse. At least it's just cookies." His expression went serious. "Tell him I said hello. He's a good kid."

"He sure is. How's your dad?"

There was a twinkle in Marcus's blue eyes. "Same as usual. He's ecstatic that I'm going to start working at the station soon."

"You're done with school already?"

"After the term finishes. I'm putting that whole thing on hold for now."

"Huh."

Marcus shrugged. "That's life. Priorities shift." He returned his gaze to the crossword.

Perry walked away feeling light but not dazed.

Chapter 42

Monday

Marcus showed up an hour later than his usual time.

"Sorry I'm late," he said, looking flustered.

"You should be sorry," Perry said. "You're going to throw off my whole day."

She filled his coffee cup two-thirds full.

"Perfect," he said. "How are the cows and chickens?"

"They're jealous of the new goats."

"You have goats?"

"That's where goat cheese comes from."

Marcus shrugged. "You learn something every day. How's your brother's friend? Kyle?"

"He's obsessed with sports trading cards. The other day, I tried to tempt him with one of my bras just to change the subject, but he only wanted to talk about his cards."

"Sounds about right for his age. I went through a cards phase myself."

"On the plus side, my brother has switched from cookies to sports cards for his dopamine hits."

"Isn't that more expensive?"

"It is, but at least my father has stopped threatening to put him on a diet."

"I'm glad things are okay."

"How's school?"

"It's a grind, but finals are coming up, and then I'm done. For now, at least. Next month, I start work at the station."

"Joining the family business."

"My mom's at a different station, but I will be working with my dad."

"Is he going to let you be on camera and talk about the weather?"

"Maybe."

"I shall begin preparations for my new shrine dedicated to Marcus Philby, Junior Weatherman."

He grinned.

Perry knew, like any good performer did, to always leave the stage on a high note. She winked at Marcus and left him to his coffee and crossword puzzle.

Chapter 43

Monday

Crossword Guy came in at his usual time. Perry filled his cup three-quarters full.

"That's exactly how much I need," he said. "Do I hear harmonica music?"

"I wouldn't call it music," Perry said. "Our prep cook has purchased a harmonica. We're trying to get him to stop, but the usual threats of violence aren't working."

"That's odd," Marcus said. "Violence is always the answer to any sort of conflict."

"I know, right?"

The harmonica sounds continued.

"I'm no music expert, but I don't think he's very good."

"I *am* a music expert, and I can tell you he is utterly terrible."

"You would know."

"He's only playing that thing to exercise his lips. He thinks it will improve his kissing skills."

"Is that something people do?"

"People kiss all the time, Marcus."

He grinned. "They don't kiss me."

"I can introduce you to Toph. He's looking for some warmup practice before the main event."

"Pass," he said.

"Don't you want to know about the main event?"

"Something tells me I don't want to know, but also that you're going to tell me anyway."

"If I haven't kissed anyone else yet, I have to kiss him on the summer solstice. In the walk-in cooler. Our cook, Donny, is going to decorate it for the event."

"On the summer solstice? But that's in three weeks."

"I know. Do you think I should get a harmonica? I wouldn't want him to outkiss me. I don't want my lips to be weak."

"Why is this happening? Did you lose a bet?"

"As with all stupid arrangements, I can't recall quite how I got myself into this one, but it's mainly because neither of us has kissed anyone before."

"You haven't...?"

"I lied when I told you I could write a juicy tell-all memoir. I have zero experience. As you may have guessed, my game is not very good. I do things like get guys to put on my pajamas and eat popcorn on my bed with my little brother present. Not very romantic."

"I'm glad."

"You are?"

"I'm glad you didn't kiss Yaro. He's got incredible lips, from what I've heard. It would be difficult for any other guy to compete with that memory."

"I suppose it would. Now my future boyfriends will have to beat Harmonica Lips."

The harmonica melody coming from the kitchen abruptly stopped, followed by a clatter and then Donny yelling about Toph finding another artistic outlet.

"That sounds like it could get ugly," Marcus said.

"I'm living in a house with both of my parents while they negotiate a divorce. Unless there's actual blood being shed back there in the kitchen, it's nothing compared to what I see on a daily basis."

"Your mom's back in town?"

Perry nodded. "It's not ideal, but they're trying to make the split amicable. Mom wants it all cleared away before the new song releases."

"I'm sorry you're going through that."

"Don't be sorry. It was a long time coming."

"I won't listen to her new song, I swear. If I hear it on the radio, I'll turn it off."

"That doesn't work. It keeps playing in your head."

"Then I'll listen, but I won't like it."

"Thanks," Perry said. "You're a good friend."

"I am?"

"So far."

Chapter 44

Monday

"No harmonica today," Marcus said.

Perry filled his coffee cup all the way.

"Donny smashed it," Perry said.

"Does that mean the bet is off?"

Perry shook her head. "It's still on. And every time we finish a meal break, Toph makes eye contact with me while applying lip balm."

Marcus squirmed in his chair. "You don't have to do it. There are rules about harassment in the workplace."

"There are rules against all the fun stuff we do." Perry shrugged. "Toph is a friend. It's just a kiss. It's a distraction from all the other stuff going on that sucks."

"Your folks are still cohabitating while they work stuff out?"

"Mom's gone back to LA. It's for the best. That's where she belongs."

"I heard the new song." Marcus wrinkled his nose. "It's terrible."

"You don't have to lie."

Marcus sighed. "Fine. It's amazing. It may be her best single ever. Can you love the art even if you don't like the artist?"

"I don't know. Can you?"

"I've still got one of Yaro's early pieces. I said I was keeping it for the investment value, but I actually like it."

"Are you guys still not talking?"

"You heard about that?"

"He took Courtney out for dinner to apologize. I don't think he was sorry, though. Just doing reputation management."

"Sounds like a Yaro Banks thing to do. I'm sorry I introduced him to you."

"Things have a way of working out in the end." She smiled. "Are you having the usual today?"

"Yes, please."

Chapter 45

Monday

That Monday, Perry filled Marcus's coffee cup right to the brim.

Marcus said, "You could probably get another drop in there if you tried."

"I could, but then you'd just dribble it all over the place with your big, clumsy hands, and I'd have to clean it up."

"My hands are a regular size, and they're not clumsy."

"Can you pick that up without spilling it?"

"Yes." He leaned forward and slurped from the top of the cup while simultaneously lifting it up.

"That's cheating," Perry said.

"I picked it up, and I didn't spill it. Just because I thought of something you didn't doesn't mean I was cheating."

"Shall I have Donny whip you up the usual?"

"Yes, please."

"Anything else?"

"The summer solstice is coming up."

"I know. It's next week."

"Any changes to your arrangement?"

"Toph has been eating well-done porkchops to strengthen his face muscles."

"If he kisses someone else before the solstice, your deal is off, right?"

"Those are the terms."

"I see." He took another sip of his coffee.

"How are finals going?"

"Not bad. I'll finish up the year with a decent grade, even though my heart's not in it. I guess I'm not like your dad. Maybe I wasn't cut out to be an engineer."

"I'm not sure he is, either. He's been writing poetry."

Marcus nearly choked on his coffee. "What?"

"You'll have to come for dinner again sometime to get a live performance and hear it for yourself."

"I'd like that." He reached into his pocket. "Speaking of your family, I went through my old sports cards, and I found these. I thought your brother and his friend might like them."

Perry took the cards. They were warm from Marcus's pocket. "Are they valuable? You should sell them if they are."

"I want Garnet and Kyle to have them."

"That's..." Perry didn't know what to say, so she refilled Crossword Guy's coffee cup and walked away.

Chapter 46

Monday (The last one.)

"It's a very special week," Marcus said.

Perry looked down at the newspaper on the table in front of him. "New design on the crossword grid?"

"I'm done with school," he said. "I'm starting at the TV station tomorrow."

"Good for you. I'd offer you a high five, but it's a fireable offense."

"Employees can make out with each other in the walk-in cooler, but giving someone a high-five is a fireable offense?"

"I don't make the rules."

Marcus gave her side eye. "I think you do. I think you and Courtney and the other waitresses are making it up as you go."

"Fine. You can have a high five, but don't let the other customers see or they'll want one, too."

Marcus held his hand low over the table. Perry touched his hand, palm to palm and fingers to fingers.

"Look at that," she said. "Our hands look nice together."

"We should try this sometime with our feet. We could do a high twenty."

Perry yanked her hand away. "Don't you dare take your shoes and socks off in the restaurant. People have been banished for far less."

Marcus grinned. "I meant at the beach."

"That would be a more appropriate venue," she said.

"What do you say? Would you like to go to the beach with me sometime? We could go to the Pier and walk around."

"And ruin the beautiful thing we have going? Our weekly breakfast date?"

"Perry, I only came in Mondays because that was the morning I didn't have classes. Starting next week, I'll have to be at work on Mondays. I could still come in for lunch, but it's a bit of a drive from the station. If there's traffic, I'd only have about five minutes to eat."

"You're not going to be here next Monday?"

"That's what I'm telling you. But maybe if you give me your phone number, we could meet up some other way."

"As friends?"

He nodded.

"Okay. Give me your phone."

He handed her his phone, and she punched in her number.

"Thanks," he said.

The bell in the kitchen rang. An order was up.

The restaurant got busy quickly. Courtney brought Marcus his bill, and he left early without saying goodbye to Perry.

Chapter 47

Day of the Summer Solstice

The special day arrived.

Donny pulled up an empty mayonnaise bucket and sat in front of Perry with a serious expression. "You don't have to kiss Toph, or anyone else for that matter." Donny rubbed his sideburns then twirled his wedding band. "I'm a grown man. I know better than to make you kids do stuff. I do have *some* self awareness."

"It's not for you. It's for Toph," Perry said. "If giving the kid one little kiss makes him feel better about himself, why wouldn't I do it?"

Toph hadn't arrived yet, and it was only the two of them in the kitchen.

Donny said, "I'd kiss him myself, but that's what got us into this mess."

"Exactly. This whole thing is all because you couldn't keep your luscious, manly lips to yourself."

"I've learned my lesson."

"Good."

Donny looked down at his wedding band and twirled it some more. "When Crossword Guy started coming in every Monday, I thought for sure you two were going to take things to the next level."

"I did, too." She looked down at the tiles and pointed her toes together. "Now I don't think I'll ever see him again."

"He hasn't called?"

"Nope. I guess he's busy at his new job."

"No man in the history of time has ever been too busy for a woman he's interested in."

Perry groaned. He was right. Donny was a goof, but when he was right, he was right.

"I blew it," she said.

"You didn't do anything wrong," Donny said. "You were honest with that boy, mostly, and you are an amazing young woman. I hope my daughter grows up to be as strong and independent as you."

Perry rolled her eyes. "Don't compare me to your new puppy, please."

"You should come over and walk her again. She likes you."

"She likes food."

"Everybody likes food. It's what keeps us in a job." He got up with a groan. "Speaking of which, I should cut the green stuff off the big block of cheese and start getting ready for the breakfast rush."

"I'll put on the coffee."

"Fresh grounds, please. No banana peels."

"Sure," she said. "It is, after all, our special day today."

Donny asked, "What time is this thing going down, anyway?"

"Courtney says two o'clock would be the best. She's really taken charge of it, and she keeps giggling about it."

"She's a funny duck, but we like her."

"Courtney says it'll be quiet up front at two o'clock, and it might be best to do it then rather than later, so it's before the next shift arrives."

"Two o'clock it is. When the coffee's ready, can you fill the red mug and bring it back here to me?"

"Will do."

Perry made coffee, tidied up the dining room, washed the face prints off the front windows, and prepared for her final shift opening as a girl who'd never been kissed.

Delilah's was busy, and the morning flew by.

It seemed to Perry like time had barely passed when Courtney handed Perry a stick of mint gum and said, "It's ten minutes to two o'clock."

Perry's muscles twitched, and her calf immediately cramped up. She stretched out the calf and chewed the gum.

Perry asked Courtney, "How's my hair? How's my makeup?"

"Good enough, but add this." Courtney handed Perry a tube of red lipstick. "By special request," she said.

Perry shook the tube. "This is for evidence, isn't it? You guys are going to check Toph for lipstick when he comes out of the cooler! You little perverts."

"Shut up and put on the lipstick. I've got another surprise."

Perry put on the lipstick. "Nice color," she said. "I'll have to reapply it after this coat gets gnawed up by the lusty badger."

Courtney took the lipstick and applied a fresh coat to her own lips. "Perfect, right?"

"It looks better on you. What's the surprise?"

Courtney did a visual check of the dining room. There were a few tables, but they were slowly finishing their meals and wouldn't need anything for a while. Then she took Perry by the hand and led her back to the kitchen.

Toph was wearing his usual apron and kitchen whites, but he'd added a bowtie to the outfit.

"Nice tie," Perry said.

Donny jumped in and said, "Thanks. It's from my wedding. I figured it would bring the kid luck."

Toph didn't say anything. He was visibly sweating.

Courtney said to the other three Delilah's employees, "As we all know, today's kiss is about reassuring Toph that he likes girls, and also to erase the memory of Donny's luscious lips from his poor young mind. No offence, Donny."

"None taken."

"What we need today is a volunteer of the female persuasion to go into the walk-in cooler with Toph."

Perry said, "Why are you being so formal? Do you want me to raise my hand or something? Is there a pledge? There'd better not be a pledge."

"My point is that the female could be any female," Courtney said. "Which is why I'm volunteering."

The other three all said, "What?"

"I haven't kissed anyone since Yaro, and I'd like a new recent kiss memory," Courtney said. "Is that okay with you, Toph? Will you take a substitute?"

"As long as it's not Donny's cousin Rhonda. She scares me." Toph wiped sweat from his brow. "You don't have to do this. It was all just a joke. I didn't think it was actually going to happen."

Courtney gave him a sidelong look. "Are you sure about that? You want to pass up your opportunity for a sure thing?"

Toph sighed and dropped his shoulders. "If it's okay with you, yeah."

Courtney shrugged. "Okay. We can call it off."

Everyone looked at Donny.

Donny said, "We'll have to think of a new stupid thing to waste time on for the next few months." He rubbed his sideburns. "I've got a few ideas that involve unusual flavor combinations."

Perry didn't know what to say. She kept pursing her lips and then rubbing her lipstick around. On some level she was quite disappointed.

Donny said, "We'd better prep for the next shift, or they'll know we were up to something." He pointed at the walk-in cooler. "Toph, go in there and take down the twinkle light decorations."

Toph saluted Donny. "Will do, boss." He practically skipped into the cooler and closed the door behind him.

Courtney said, "I'll help." She walked over to the cooler, flicked off the light, went in, and closed the door behind her.

Perry and Donny looked at each other.

"It's happening," Donny said.

They looked at the door, which remained closed.

Perry said, "Do you think we could hear anything if we put our ears to the door?"

"There's a lot of insulation, plus the compressors are going, but I think we need to try."

They both ran over to the door and pressed their ears against it.

Donny asked, "Can you hear anything?"

Perry whispered, "I think I hear giggling. Shh."

There was a knock at the back door.

Both Donny and Perry ran away from the cooler door guiltily.

Perry yanked open the back door. "We weren't doin' nothin'," she said, expecting to see someone from the afternoon shift.

Marcus Philby stood on the other side of the door, his hands in his pockets.

"Hi," he said. "I came in the front door, but nobody was out there. I figured you might be back here."

"It's two o'clock. Aren't you supposed to be at work? Don't tell me you got fired already."

"I got off early. When I was here on Monday, Courtney followed me outside and told me to come back today, at two o'clock." He leaned over and glanced around. "Is she here?"

"She's in the cooler, making a man out of Toph."

Marcus's eyes widened. "She is?"

Donny had a coughing fit. "She'd better not be," he said. "They're just kissing. That's all."

Perry said to Donny, "You'd better check that boy for lipstick when he comes out."

Donny waved both hands. "No, thank you."

Perry turned back to Marcus. "You're here," she said. "I thought I'd never see you again. Not until one night when I turned on my TV and found my favorite weatherman gone, replaced with a younger model."

"I should have called," he said. "But you know me. I don't call. I just show up, whether you want me to or not."

Donny came over and said, "I hate to interrupt this adorable exchange, but get out of my kitchen. Perry, you're off shift now. Maggie just walked in the front."

"But I'm not off for a few more hours," Perry said.

"Courtney changed the schedule," Donny said. "Take off that apron and go do something fun with Crossword Guy. That's an order."

Marcus said, "I've got the rest of the afternoon free, and I'm driving the you-know-what." He gestured to his father's sports car, which was parked next to the trash bins in the alley.

Perry took off her waitress apron and tossed it on the prep counter.

She stepped outside into the warm summer breeze and pulled the door shut behind her.

"Marcus, how do you feel about my lipstick?"

"It's a bold color."

"How would you feel about wearing it?"

"What?"

She grabbed his face with both hands and kissed him. The kiss landed almost squarely on his mouth. It wasn't bad for a first kiss.

Chapter 48

Later that Evening

Perry and Marcus sat on a log on the beach, watching the sun set on the longest day of the year.

"This day feels like it's been a week long," Perry said.

"Hey," Marcus said, sounding offended.

"But also like ten minutes," Perry said.

Marcus reached over and looped his fingers through hers. "Our hands do look good together. Should we take off our shoes and socks and try for a high twenty?"

"Save something for the next date," she said.

He chuckled and squeezed her hand.

They'd been hanging out for seven hours, and there wasn't too much left to say—for that day, anyway.

The sun dropped to the halfway point.

Marcus said, "Remember that time you kissed me in the alley by the dumpsters? That was the most romantic thing anyone's ever done for me."

"My dad says I inherited my grandmother's flair for dramatic moments."

They were interrupted by a man approaching with a large camera.

Perry turned her face to hide it in Marcus's shoulder. "Make him go away," she whimpered. "I can't deal with this today."

She heard the man asking, in broken English, for Marcus to take a picture of him and his wife.

Perry pulled away from Marcus and laughed. "I thought it was one of those horrible photographers from the gossip sites."

Marcus got up, took the camera from the man, and snapped his photograph.

The man told Marcus that his girlfriend was very pretty, and she looked familiar.

"She is pretty," Marcus said. "Do you ever eat at Delilah's? She works there. That must be where you know her from."

The man said he didn't think so, but he took the camera, thanked them both, and walked away with his wife.

Perry looked into Marcus's eyes. She lifted off his glasses so she could see them better.

"You let that man think I was your girlfriend."

"Do you want to be my girlfriend?"

"I don't know. What are the rules?"

"No more making plans to kiss your coworkers in the walk-in cooler."

"Fair enough," she said. "You can't kiss any of your coworkers in the sound booth or whatever."

"I wouldn't want to." He ran his fingertip down the center of her forehead and her nose. "What are your other rules for your boyfriend?"

"You can't sell my pictures or personal information to the gossip websites or magazines."

Marcus frowned. "Darn. There goes my retirement plan. But if that's how it's going to be, I can agree to those terms. What else?"

"Dinner at my house once a week, and if we have weekend plans, we bring my brother half the time."

"Your brother can join us all the time."

Perry pulled back. "Do you want to be my boyfriend or not?"

He laughed. "Okay. You figure out how much Garnet time is the right amount of time."

"And Kyle has to come along sometimes, too."

"Deal breaker." He got to his feet.

Perry grabbed his hand and pulled him back down to the log. She put his glasses back on his face.

"I accept your terms," he said.

"Do you have any more for me?"

"None that I feel like saying out loud," Marcus said.

"Are you implying that you don't want me to have any more pajama sleepovers with Yaro Banks?"

"I didn't want to say it."

"It won't happen again. He came by the cafe last week and dropped off my artwork. We shook hands and agreed to carry on as acquaintances rather than friends."

"I'm sorry nothing happened with your artwork."

"Don't be. And what do you mean, nothing? I've got a show coming up."

"You do?"

"It's at Delilah's. You're invited, of course."

"I wouldn't miss it for the world."

"Uh-oh." She turned her face toward the ocean. "We missed it. The sun has disappeared. Once it starts to dip down, it happens so fast."

"We haven't missed it," Marcus said.

"We haven't?"

He pulled off his glasses.

"We haven't missed anything," he said, and he kissed her.

Chapter 49

Perry Langtree's debut art exhibition, entitled Mother's Monsters, didn't happen until the middle of December.

The extra time allowed Perry to create several new creatures out of scraps of felt, old clothes, and found objects.

The art show opening, held at Delilah's after closing time, was a small affair, attended mostly by staff, friends, and a few people from the businesses on Baker Street.

The Russian guy who'd run the pop-up ice cream shop during the summer was there, with his little Chihuahua, Duke. He looked over all the hand-sewn creatures then selected one and pulled out his wallet.

Perry was so overcome with excitement over selling her first piece of art that she was unable to ring up the sale. Her hands were shaking, and she couldn't remember the code for ringing in off-menu items. Courtney had to take over.

Courtney said to the man, "You'd better not be planning to give this to your dog as a chew toy."

In a thick Russian accent, he replied, "Is not for dog. Too many small pieces. Choke dog." He held up the hand-stitched, one-of-a-kind creature. "Is for Christmas tree."

"Yes," Courtney said, matching his accent. "Is for Christmas tree."

After the man left with the wrapped-up creature, Courtney said to Perry, "You know the accent is fake, right? I've heard him talking to Justine at the Quick Stop, and he just has a regular Russian accent."

"That's a great act he's got going," Perry said. "It gives me an idea. Tomorrow, I'm going to wear one of my mom's wigs and try out a new Russian personality on the customers. Can you go along with it and call me Natasha?"

"You know I will."

"And you can practice your fake German." Perry started making sounds that felt German to her.

Courtney elbowed Perry to be quiet. "Shh. We have another customer."

An energetic woman with long, dark hair approached, holding two of the monsters. "This little man needs to come home with me," she said, waving the orange one. "It looks exactly like my cat, Muffins."

Perry recognized the woman as one of their regular customers, Megan Gardenia. She and her sister ran the flower shop down the street. Their mother had been friends with one of the other waitresses, Maggie, for years.

"Sold," Perry said. "That one does have a feline energy."

Megan Gardenia held up the green one. "And this one is going to my boyfriend's office." She examined it more closely. "Are those real human teeth it's holding?"

"That one's called the Tooth Fairy," Perry said. "It's holding real teeth, but not from a human."

"Good enough," the florist said. "My boyfriend is a dentist. He can use this to scare kids into brushing more." She cackled.

The woman standing next to her, Tina Gardenia, also a regular customer at Delilah's, rolled her eyes. "I apologize for my sister," Tina said. "She has a strange sense of humor."

Perry threw her hands in the air. "As long as she's buying my artwork, I'd say her sense of humor is perfect!"

Courtney rang in the sale, wrapped up the monsters, and thanked the sisters for stopping in.

By the end of the night, all twenty-five of the monsters had been sold.

Courtney locked the door and dimmed the lights. A small group of family and friends stayed behind and gathered in one of the large booths. They drank eggnog and enjoyed the Christmas treats Donny and Toph had prepared. Donny's wife was there, and she'd brought in a selection of handmade pottery as gifts for everyone.

Courtney snuggled up close to Toph, who put his arm around her shoulders. Ever since their summer solstice encounter in the walk-in cooler, from which Toph had emerged *covered* in red lipstick, the two had been an item. They couldn't keep their hands off each other. What a couple of lusty badgers! Donny had been threatening to install a window in the walk-in cooler door "for safety," and also to keep the rest of the crew from walking in on things they didn't want to see.

Perry gazed happily across the booth at her father and brother. The Langtree boys were laughing and looking through some new sports cards Garnet had picked up that day.

Garnet was now aware of the true results of his paternity test. The family had gone through a rough patch, but now it seemed like the two of them were closer than ever.

Garnet had hit a growth spurt in the fall, and the strangest thing had happened. His jet-black hair had lightened to a softer brown, and his face shape had changed. He looked, more than ever, like the genetic offspring of Dale Langtree. It was uncanny. It had also kept the press from creating yet another scandal.

Crossword Guy, also known as Marcus Philby, returned from the washroom and slid in next to Perry. "Great debut show," he said, squeezing her hand. "I'm so proud of you. Not many people have what it takes to be a sell-out."

"Thanks," she said. "I didn't even go through a *precious artiste* state before hitting sell-out status."

"That's because you're so talented."

"I didn't get to use any of the red stickers you bought," she said, pouting. "People started taking my monsters right off the walls, and I didn't have the heart to tell them the pieces had to stay up until the end of the month."

"You've got more at home, right? I'll swing by early tomorrow and help you put more of them on display. Then we'll change the prices so they're ten times as much."

"Good idea," she said. "Maybe only twice as much. They're just scraps of fabric."

"Don't sell yourself short," Marcus said. "They're all originals, just like you."

Perry said, "You know what else is original? My mom's new Christmas song."

"I heard it," Marcus said. "It's terrible."

"Don't lie."

"It's the most amazing Christmas song ever recorded," he said. "A future classic, for sure. But not as good as Lana Langtree's version of Santa Baby."

"My grandma's coming to visit soon. Are you excited about meeting her?"

"Not as excited as my dad is. Are you sure you want to have the Philby family over at your house for the big day?"

"Absolutely. It's going to be the best Christmas ever. Kyle's going to join us this year. If he asks you to smell his hand, don't."

"I've learned," Marcus said. "Anything I should know about meeting your grandma?"

"Just that she will squeeze your cheeks like this." Perry squeezed his cheeks.

"That's not so bad," he said with his fish lips.

"And she will kiss you right on the mouth."

He raised his eyebrows. "Is she really that friendly in real life?"

"Not always, but who could resist these luscious lips?" She kissed him, but only briefly. Her family and friends were right there.

Marcus leaned in and whispered, "That tasted like another one."

"Shh," she said, then, "Meet me inside the walk-in cooler in five minutes."

"Why?"

"It's full of mistletoe and twinkle lights."

"But isn't it cold?"

She looked at him, eyebrows raised.

"Oh," he said.

She winked and squeezed out of the booth, saying she had to check on something in the kitchen.

Marcus managed to wait four and a half minutes before excusing himself as well.

If you enjoyed this novel, you'll love Angie Pepper's other books set on Baker Street, featuring more great romantic comedy plus guest appearances by your favorite characters!

For a full list of titles, visit the author's website at **www.angelapepper.com**

Thanks for reading!

* 9 7 8 1 9 9 0 3 6 7 2 7 4 *